STAR CROSSED

TAURUS EYES

BONNIE HEARN HILL

RP|TEENS
PHILADELPHIA · LONDON

Library of Congress Control Number: 2009940139

ISBN 978-0-7624-3671-2

Cover and interior design by Ryan Hayes
Typography: Chronicle Text, Knockout, Affair
Cover image: iStock

Published by Running Press Teens, an imprint of
Running Press Book Publishers
2300 Chestnut Street
Philadelphia, PA 19103-4371

Visit us on the web!

www.runningpress.com

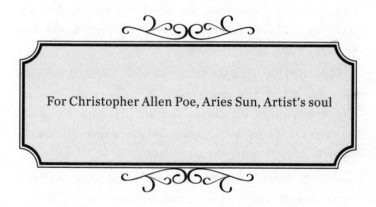

For Christopher Allen Poe, Aries Sun, Artist's soul

What's your sign?
Check out ours.

Jeremy, a hot **Taurus,** and what **Taurus** isn't? It's about the eyes. And the passion. And the sense of purpose. And the eyes. I think he likes me, but we have the same topic for our class article: a dead folksinger whose spirit just might be haunting Monterey. I would like to think our stars are lined up, but it doesn't look good. That Taurus is not going to change his focused, fixed ways for me.

Sean Baylor, the **Gemini** folksinger who is responsible for all of the excitement. A sailboat accident in the sixties ended his career and his life. Now his ghost is supposed to be back, which really takes his sign's natural curiosity to the next level.

Henry Jaffa, Aquarius, the famous paranormal investigative writer leading our summer writing workshop. If I get my way, he will be my new writing mentor. He won't make rapid decisions, though. Aquarius needs to think things through. Just ask me.

Vanessa, an **Aries.** Sexy, clueless, and absolutely after Jeremy. And the Ram of the zodiac, even a clueless one, usually gets what she goes after. But she is so not a writer. Why is she really here?

Candice, my **Virgo** roommate from Colorado. Rich, gorgeous, and a perfectionist true to her sign. Although

Virgos can be critical, she is kind about the way she does it. And she is the social center of our lives.

Tatiyana, a trendy, hard-working **Capricorn** with a violet streak in her black hair, she is Vanessa's long-suffering roommate. This sign is all about the work and all about making the money, but it is also Earth, which means she's stable. I hope she is because Vanessa certainly isn't.

Dirk, Sagittarius. Cute ponytail guy from the United Kingdom, with accent to match. He is Jeremy's roommate and seems really into Candice, or maybe Vanessa. Or is it Tatiyana? The guy gets around as Sadges do, both geographically, and sometimes in their personal lives.

Nathan, my first serious crush. He's a **Leo,** and is always drawing people to him, making it look easy. Do I really want to see him again?

Mercedes, Libra reporter who once interviewed Baylor. Air sign Libra can see both sides of a situation, but is she trying to get at the truth or to hide it?

Ren Baylor, Sean Baylor's emotional **Cancer** sister, willing to use her influence to cause serious problems for me. Cancer cares deeply about family, and this one is none too happy about the publicity her dead brother's ghost is receiving.

Eldon, make that **Cookie, Scorpio** drummer who performed with Sean Baylor on the night of Baylor's death. What secrets about that night is this guy hiding?

Christopher Ritter (Critter), a laid-back party guy who rarely takes off his shades. A **Pisces**, all the way, he is everybody's friend, except maybe his own.

And me, **Logan McRae**, a living-in-my-head **Aquarius**, the same as Jaffa. This is my chance. I need to convince this mentor to many that I am worth mentoring as well, and I might be able to outsmart Jeremy and actually get my article published. The only problem is that I don't want to outsmart Jeremy. I want to work together. And, yes, I want our stars to be aligned. Maybe they will be if I just give it a little more time. And if I can find out what really happened to Sean Baylor.

WELCOME TO *Fearless Astrology, Volume 2.* USE THE
KNOWLEDGE THAT YOU GAIN HERE WISELY. IT WILL
SERVE YOU WELL THROUGH TIMES OF JOY AND TIMES
OF CHALLENGE.

—Fearless Astrology

The ghost tour leader was ten minutes late. I didn't
care. Although I'd put on a good show, I, Logan
McRae, was miserable. My mom had left for another
golf tour. My two best girlfriends were on vacation. Worst of
all, I'd lost a guy I really cared about, and in a very public way.

So, no, I wasn't all that interested in Monterey's ghosts,
its Cannery Row or the tantalizing fragrance of the sea air.

Breaking up with someone you care about can do that to
you. *Times of challenge.* You got that one right, *Fearless.*

I glanced up at the moon. It would be in the emotional

sign of Cancer for another day-and-a-half. No way was I going to let that moon influence my wallowing. Time to focus on the good.

Here I was with a fellowship to the California State University at Monterey Bay for outstanding high school journalism students. My new roommate, Candice Armstrong, and I would soon join twelve other kids to take a tour of Monterey's supposedly haunted downtown. Our guest lecturer was none other than Henry Jaffa. *The* Henry Jaffa. Bestselling paranormal investigative journalist, who donated time and money to help young writers. That Henry Jaffa.

He had sat right across the table from me at dinner, and I'd barely been able to eat. All of us had just kept staring at him. Except for Vanessa Lowe, that is, a pushy, curvy brunette from Texas. She'd hammered him with questions and flattery from the clam chowder right through the halibut parmesan. She was still talking while Jaffa tried to swallow a few spoonfuls of his melting hazelnut gelato.

Candice and I stood together outside the restaurant waiting for the tour bus. We both wore jeans and our black T-shirts with *Writers Camp* in purple letters on the front. I had to admit neither of us filled them out the way Vanessa did hers.

Candice was about my size, except on her, thin looked good. She had shiny, streaked rich-girl hair and a way of carrying herself that made her appear taller than she was. In a word, she was elegant. A steady Earth sign, I guessed, with a cool exterior that made me guess Capricorn somewhere in her chart. Dirk, a cute British guy with a long ponytail, had been checking her out at dinner, but she told me she had a boyfriend back home in Colorado. She also had two older sisters, who were, she said, a royal pain. I had worried that I would get stuck with a Vanessa-type roommate and was glad that Candice seemed so calm and easygoing.

The two redheads from New York were twins and, of course, roomed together. Christopher Ritter, who introduced himself as Critter, was a stoner with blond curls and a laid-back way of speaking that must have taken a lot of practice to pull off. I didn't have names for the others yet.

"Could you believe the wicked witch of west Texas?" Candice asked. "With Vanessa in the workshop, we'll be lucky to even talk to Jaffa."

"With him," I said. "I don't think it's about the talking."

Candice nodded. "It's about the writing. Let's hope she sucks at it."

"Or that she's easily distracted." On the other side of the walkway, Vanessa chatted up a cute guy in a khaki jacket with a matching bag over his shoulder. "If that guy's part of our workshop, she might not be that interested in Jaffa after all."

"He's cute, but he isn't a bestselling writer," Candice said.

"He is hot, though," I replied.

Just then, a dark green bus pulled up, and a woman with a gray bob stepped out. Her face was younger than her hair, her eyes hidden behind pink-tinted glasses.

"Writers Camp tour boarding now," she called out in a

starched, professional voice. "We leave in ten minutes. Mr. Jaffa, please come forward."

Jaffa emerged from the crowd and climbed up the stairs.

The cute guy was next. Then came the African American chick who'd sat on the other side of Jaffa at dinner. As she swung up the steps to the bus, her violet tie-dyed scarf blew behind her. It matched the streak of hair falling over one eye.

"Let's go," Candice said, and we began to run.

She got there first. Then, finally, I was aboard. Ahead of me, Henry Jaffa sat next to a window paging through a guidebook. His bushy gray hair caught the lights of the bus. The seat beside him was empty. This was my chance. I started toward him.

Then I felt someone hit me from behind. In the back. Hard.

As I fought to maintain my balance, Vanessa gave me a final shove, pushed ahead of me, and claimed the seat beside Jaffa.

A hand on the other side of the aisle shot out and grabbed mine. I looked up into riveting eyes the color of the sea. The noise of the others blurred into a steady hum. It was the cute guy who'd been talking to Vanessa outside.

He was about my age with hair so straight and shiny black that I immediately thought about my own auburn curls, no doubt hopelessly frizzed by the sea air. Although our connection must have lasted only moments, time stretched out. Then slowly, he pulled me down in the seat next to him.

Finally, the sound in my head switched back on. I heard

the chatter of the others and was able to remove my hand from his.

"Thank you," I said. "I guess I tripped." The words fell out of me clunky and stupid.

"What's your name?"

"Logan."

"I'm Jeremy." His voice was husky, yet soft. "Jeremy Novack."

"And you're part of the Writers Camp too?"

He opened his jacket, pointed at his shirt, identical to mine. "My plane was late. I just got in."

"Where are you from?"

"Jersey," he said. "I'm sorry I missed the dinner, but I can't believe I bothered to show up for this sham."

"They're doing it because Jaffa's next book is going to be about ghost sightings," I said.

"He needs to stick to the investigative stuff. You don't believe any of the ghost stories are real, do you?"

"I don't know." Those eyes of his made it almost impossible for me to remember my name, let alone anything else.

"It's hype."

Taurus. He had to be that fixed Bull of the Zodiac. I could guess his opinion of astrology.

The silver-haired tour guide stepped inside the bus.

"Is everyone aboard? Our first stop will be a bar and restaurant that has two ghosts."

Jeremy sighed.

Ahead and to the other side of us, I watched Jaffa nod. Beside him, Vanessa paged through what looked like a well used booklet. She'd obviously done her Monterey-lore homework.

"Big deal," Jeremy whispered to me. "All that stuff's easy to fake."

"The female ghost at the restaurant leaves salt in the wineglasses," Vanessa piped up.

Jaffa looked intrigued. "Monterey is full of legends and mysteries," he said. "That's one of the reasons I agreed to come here."

"Sean Baylor is another one." Vanessa glanced up from her book with a superior smile. "He was a folk singer who almost made it big in the late sixties. Some believe his spirit still occupies the restaurant where he drank before he went out on his boat that last time after the Monterey Pop Festival."

"There's no proof that Baylor is a ghost," Jeremy said. Then to me, he whispered, "Do you see what I mean about this stuff?"

Before I could reply, the tour guide said, "Well, his sailboat was found deserted in a storm. There's no way he could have survived."

"So that means he decided to stick around and haunt old Monterey?"

The woman flashed him a condescending smile. "There's no way we can know which spirits remain, or why. And, for your information, this is one of the most popular walking tours in Monterey."

"Well, have fun with your popular walking tour." He stood, said "Nice meeting you, Logan," stepped across me, and headed down the aisle toward the door.

"Wait," our tour guide shouted as he brushed past her. "This bus leaves in five minutes. It isn't going to wait for you."

"That's all right." He looked back at me again. I felt the connection and realized I couldn't stay in my seat.

"Logan," Candice called from behind me. "What are you doing?"

"I'll be right back," I said. Then I hurried past the guide, got off the bus, and started after him.

"Jeremy, wait."

He stopped, turned his head, and gave me that look again. "You'd better get back on the bus."

"Not without you," I said. "I know how hard you must have worked to get this fellowship. How can you walk away from it? How can you walk away from Henry Jaffa?"

He pulled his jacket closer and met my gaze. "I can walk away from anyone, if I have to."

I felt a chill and forced myself to ignore his words. "But you don't have to. Please come back on that bus with me."

"No way. I have to check in at the college, and I'm up to here with the ghost stuff."

"All right. If that's the way you want it." I felt like a fool for chasing after him. Slowly, I turned away. This was the smartest thing I'd done all day. Just walk back to the bus.

"Logan, don't go."

He was right behind me. I could feel his breath on my neck.

I whirled around and found myself face-to-face with him. "What?"

For the first time since he'd grabbed my hand back in the bus, he smiled.

"Let's ditch the tour and get something to eat."

"I can't."

"Why not?"

Because Henry Jaffa was on that bus. Because the beginning of the fellowship I'd fought like hell for was on that bus. Because regardless of how hot Jeremy was, I couldn't blow my dream.

"I'm sorry," I said. "I really wish . . ."

"Three minutes," announced the tour guide. She'd stepped outside the bus and was glaring at us now. "Two minutes, forty-five seconds. Are you two boarding, or would you like to walk back to the college?"

"I'll walk," Jeremy shouted back at her.

I ran for the bus.

The doors whooshed shut behind me.

The bus driver hit the gas, and I had to grab the back of his seat to steady myself. Our guide slid behind him. I made my way to the seats Jeremy and I had occupied earlier. When I saw his empty one next to the window, I felt unreasonably sad.

I'd made the right choice, though. This fellowship could

change my life. I looked up to where Henry Jaffa sat. It was only then that I realized that Vanessa was still occupying the outside seat. She gave me a smirk and then she turned back to Jaffa.

Oh great. My first night in Monterey, and I already had an enemy.

NOTES TO SELF

For some reason, Vanessa hates me. When we had to introduce ourselves on the bus and tell where we were from, she made fun of my answer. I'd said Terra Bella Beach and explained it was about ninety minutes south between here and Santa Barbara. "I can tell you're from California, Logan," she'd said with a condescending smile. "You give directions by how long it takes to get to a place." I didn't like the way she looked at me; I didn't like the laughter of the others. I especially didn't like that Jeremy wasn't in the seat beside me. So, yes, I have an enemy, a Fire sign, I'll bet. Tomorrow is our first day in class, and I'd better be ready for her.

HAMLET WAS A LIBRA
By Logan McRae

"To be or not to be?" With all of his wondering and all of his questioning, Hamlet had to be a Libra. They frequently have trouble making up their minds. His love for beauty—think Ophelia—is par for the course for one ruled by Venus. There's a lot of talk from this Air sign, too, and Libras are known for their communication skills.

I stop writing. The talk could also mean that Hamlet was a Gemini or even a Sadge. And with all of that karmic family emotional stuff, he could have been a Scorpio or a Cancer. The emoting on stage could be the sign of a Leo or Aries. Many Capricorns have unsettled childhoods. He certainly qualified in that department. Then, there are emotionally stuck Pisces, pondering Aquarius, perfectionist Virgo, and uncompromising Taurus. When I first discovered Fearless Astrology, I would have made that easy assumption about Libra. Now I realize that what I need to do with my article is to show how the Sun sign is really only the beginning. Yes. Instead of trying to argue the sign of a fictional character, I'm going to show how impossible it is to use only the Sun to understand someone, fictional or otherwise.

Jaffa is known for his interest in subjects off the beaten track. I can't wait to see what he thinks about astrology.

2

THOSE WITH THE SUN IN TAURUS CAN'T HIDE THEIR
EMOTIONS, NOT WITH THOSE EXPRESSIVE EYES.
ALTHOUGH NOT GUARDED LIKE SCORPIO, NOR
SPARKLING LIKE AQUARIUS, NOR IMPISH LIKE GEMINI,
TAURUS EYES ARE PENETRATING AND THOUGHTFUL.
AND THEY CAN MAKE YOU FEEL AS IF THEY ARE SEEING
INTO YOUR VERY SOUL.

—*Fearless Astrology*

s soon as we returned to the dorms after the
ghost tour, I'd gotten to work on my laptop and
done some hasty investigating.

Online search: Henry Jaffa, author, February 14.

Online answer: Sun Sign, Aquarius.

Make that, another Aquarius. Another analyzer. Another

want-to-change-the-worlder. Another same sign as mine. Please let him like my astrology slant. I had reworked my article outline. It was now called "Beyond the Sun: Understanding True Character through Astrology." I threw the "True" in there because of what I had discovered when trying to define Hamlet as a Sun sign only. The change would make my paper deeper, and I couldn't wait to get started on it. With Henry Jaffa on my side—which he would soon be—maybe I'd have a chance to publish my piece.

I stumbled out of bed into a day that smelled fresh and full of promise. The sea air and waves had soothed me to sleep last night, and I woke with the realization that my life was not over just because Vanessa from TexASS disliked me. Jaffa was the one who mattered. He had mentioned that he took a morning run on the beach every day, and I was tempted to do the same. Not yet, though. It would be too obvious.

After looking at my class information, I matched faces to names. The redheaded twins from New York were Darla and Andrea. Critter's roommate with the shaved head was Brad, known as Brad Dog.

Only a mile from Monterey Bay, the campus was located on what used to be Fort Ord, an army base that closed in the mid-nineties.

"I've heard that this place is haunted," Candice said as we walked to class. Her hair was perfect, in spite of the breeze, and although she had tried to help me with mine, it was impossible and frizzy as ever.

"Monterey is big on ghosts," I told her. "That's probably why Jaffa's so interested in teaching here."

"That's my article topic," she said. "The ghosts of downtown Monterey. My oldest sister is an English major, but she's never been in a national anthology."

Neither had I, and as she spoke, I realized that we were all in competition here, only that the competition was more blatant than it was in school. Only one of us, if that, would end up in the anthology.

"I think it's a great topic," I said.

"Your new friend certainly doesn't seem interested in ghosts." Candice nudged me. "Speaking of . . ."

I turned to see Jeremy behind us on the path.

"Hey, Logan."

Wearing the Writers Camp tee and a pair of jeans, he was even better looking in the morning light. The breeze that was already cutting through my layered clothing didn't seem to bother him.

"Hi," I called back, and he hurried to catch up with us.

Candice gave me a knowing grin. "See you," she said.

That left Jeremy and me face to face. The wind terrorizing my hair seemed to only toy with his.

He pushed a chunk out of his eyes and said, "I was hoping to run into you."

"You were?"

"Yeah." He moved so close to me that I was afraid to

breathe. "I'm sorry I was an ass last night."

I started to tell him he wasn't an ass, but amended it to, "That's okay."

"It was a long flight from Jersey," he said, "and, to be honest, I'm not into this Ghostbuster stuff."

"Then why'd you want to study with Jaffa?" I asked. "Didn't you know about his new project?"

"Sure, I knew. But he's still Henry Jaffa, and I'd give anything to work with him."

At last, common ground.

"Me too." I tried to slow my voice and my heartbeat. "What's your topic?"

"Sean Baylor. I'm going to prove he isn't just your basic Monterey ghost legend." His smile was pure, fixed Earth. "What's yours?"

Before I could decide whether or not to admit my fascination with astrology, Vanessa came rushing up to us. Make that, to him. She wore her oversize glasses like a headband.

"There you are, Jeremy. Hurry up. I saved you a seat. Oh, hi, Logan." She squinted at my yellow hoodie, reached up for her shades, and slid them down over her eyes. "You're certainly bright this morning."

I took advantage of my analytical Aquarian nature and decided that there was no reason to strangle her just then.

Instead I said, "No need to rush. There are only twelve of us."

"Works for me," Jeremy said. "In that case, let's get something to eat, maybe some coffee."

Food again. He had to be a Taurus, just like my brownie-loving English teacher at home.

"Afraid I can't, hon," Vanessa said in a sugary drawl. "Henry just went in, and I need to talk to him."

Henry? How blatant could she be?

"See you," Jeremy said.

"Okay." I took a deep breath and walked into the building alone.

⁓♆⁓

I had learned from an early age that, in any classroom, there are front-row kids and back-row kids. Since discovering *Fearless Astrology*, I'd started suspecting that a lot of the front-row kids were Fire signs, and a lot of the back-row kids were Water signs—with Air and Earth signs chiming in from various corners of the room.

Watery, emotional Pisces, Cancer, and Scorpio tended to hide, the way curly haired Critter and the shy brunette with long straight-cut bangs were doing, in the back of the room. The Air signs, Aquarius, Gemini, and Libra, tended to talk, so they didn't care where they sat. The Earth signs of Taurus, Virgo, and Capricorn were so Fixed and reluctant to change that they didn't care either—as long as it was the same seat they had occupied the last time. Fire signs Aries, Leo, and Sagittarius, tended to blaze their way to the front of any room lucky enough to have them in it. Or so they thought.

Sure enough, Vanessa was front and center, just opposite Jaffa's podium. Candice sat at the end of the front row.

The back row was empty except for Tatiyana, the girl with the purple streak. She had made little horizontal cuts into her T-shirt—the seams, sleeves, and a couple of rows down the front—and wore it over a violet tank. Jeremy would probably end up hiding out back there, no matter how many seats Vanessa "saved" for him in front. For a moment I considered doing the same. Then I glanced up at Jaffa already at his desk. He wore a black turtleneck and jeans, his hair as untamed as ever.

He spotted me, and a wide smile spread across his professorish face. *The* Henry Jaffa was grinning at me as if we were old friends.

I took a deep breath, walked to the front of the room, continued the eye contact and said, "Good morning."

"Hi," Jaffa replied. "You're Logan, right?"

I nodded and tried to forget that I was talking to one of the most famous writers in the country—a writer whose true-crime book on a strangler was going to be turned into a made-for-TV movie.

"Yes, I . . ."

"Have a seat." He motioned in the general direction of the front row. I slid down into the seat beside my roomie Candice.

"Wow," she whispered.

I didn't dare look at Vanessa. I couldn't begin to turn my head to see if Jeremy had come in.

"Shall we get started?" Jaffa said. "As you may know, I taught high school journalism prior to my writing career. I learned that a good journalist needs to do only three things in order to succeed. Be honest, be accurate, and be a good listener. That may be the toughest job of all, but if you listen, really listen, the other two rules will take care of themselves."

I realized I was nodding.

"So you agree, Logan?" he asked.

I froze. I managed to nod again. "Yes." My throat felt as if I'd swallowed sandpaper.

"Before we go on," Jaffa said, "I'm sure you've all heard about the young adult anthology I'm editing."

Had I ever. He was going to donate the proceeds to a literacy group—definitely a generous Aquarian gesture.

"So, what about it, Henry?" rude Vanessa asked.

"Because one of us might be in it," Jeremy said.

My face was so hot that I didn't dare turn around.

"That's right." Jaffa replied as if he'd heard my silent question. "I have permission from the publisher to include one student piece. I hope it comes from one of you. So, now, please turn in your article ideas."

I noticed Vanessa scribbling something on a notebook page. Had she really failed to prepare for this workshop?

It didn't matter now. I passed my sheet of paper toward the front of the room. Vanessa finished writing, ran to Jaffa's desk, and slammed hers on top of the pile.

He didn't seem to notice.

"Here's what we're going to do," he said. "I believe the best way to hone your author voice is to get out of your comfort zone."

Then, he grabbed the pile of papers from his desk, and tossed them up in the air.

"My topic!" Vanessa shouted.

"It's here. Now, each of you pick up the paper closest to you."

I reached down and picked up the neatly typed page that had slid under my desk.

"Ew," Candice said, looking down at hers. "I don't know anything about the Civil War."

"I do," Tati said. "But how to be a Broadway star? Give me a break."

"That's mine." Vanessa's voice was shrill.

"My point exactly," Jaffa said. "Would you all read your topics, starting with you, Logan."

I looked down at the page in my hands, evenly formatted into columns of type.

"Sean Baylor: Legend and Myth."

"That's mine." Jeremy's voice rang out from behind me.

I turned around. His expression was pure anger.

"It's Logan's now."

"But I never even heard of the guy," I said. "My subject is astrology."

"Well, I have it now," Vanessa said. "I can't imagine anything more boring."

"And I've got the downtown ghosts of Monterey." Jeremy sounded disgusted. "I can't . . ."

"Class!" Jaffa rose from his desk, as if pleased by our annoyance. "We write in order to discover. Please remember that. To discover. This exercise will make you better writers, I promise. And, yes, it will get each of you out of your comfort zone."

Forget my comfort zone. How was I going to show what I could do as an astrology writer? That was how I had planned to impress Jaffa. Just as *Fearless Astrology* had hooked me, I had been certain my topic (now in the hands of Vanessa Clueless) would hook him. There had to be a way. Of course. I needed to write about Sean Baylor from an *astrological* perspective. That was it.

When the class ended, everyone was still grumbling.

Jeremy caught up with me outside. "You turned me down twice. I thought I'd try for coffee this time."

I felt a little shiver and looked up into those riveting eyes again. *Taurus eyes*, I was betting.

Then, I glanced down at the cup in his hand. "You must be addicted."

"I'm taking that as a yes," he said. "For the coffee, I mean."

"Sounds good," I managed to reply.

We stopped at the snack bar, ordered, and took our drinks out onto the patio with its glimpse of the ocean. Even in summer, the air this close to the water was chilly. My senses seemed to slow down, as if photographing every moment. The biting cold breeze through my hoodie, the warm paper cup in my hands. Gull cries. The smell of coffee mixed with a soapy, masculine scent when he moved beside me.

"Beautiful," he said. "Can you believe how close the beach is? I'm going to spend the rest of the afternoon out there."

"It's really isolated," I said, "not like the beach at home."

"I like the whole place. I could move here tomorrow."

I loved the thoughtful, sincere way he talked, the careful manner in which he seemed to choose his words. "Would you do that?"

He nodded, and the breeze tangled his hair. "I graduated early and was accepted to college for the fall semester. But I wouldn't let that stand in the way of something I wanted."

"Do you mean . . . ?" Was he actually saying that he'd consider going to school here?

While I was still trying to figure that one out, he said, "Jaffa had no right to scramble our topics."

Where had that come from?

"Maybe he knows something we don't," I said. "Maybe getting out of our comfort zones will make us better writers, the way he says it will."

"I doubt it." He took a swallow of coffee and moved closer to me. "You don't care about Sean Baylor, do you?"

"Not really," I admitted. "I don't know anything about him."

"That makes it simple. You don't want to write about Baylor, and I do."

I tried hard not to sound defensive. "I care about my topic, too, Jeremy, but a good writer should be able to write about anything, don't you think?"

"Not if he's trying to get published in a national anthology. I've studied Baylor's music all of my life. I want to be a singer too."

"You're not an English major?" I asked.

"I'm a musician. My article in that anthology will be read by a lot of people. All I need is for the right person to read it."

So he was hoping the anthology would launch his music career. His dreams were even bigger than mine. That made me like him more.

"Everyone in the class wants to be in the anthology," I said. "I certainly do."

He grinned, and his face seemed to light up. "Cool. Friendly competition, then."

"Friendly competition," I said, happy that we'd avoided an argument.

"I'm still going to write my article on Baylor."

"How can you do that?"

He looked down at his cup, then at me. "I was thinking that we could just trade topics."

"Jaffa would kick us out of class. I have to write about Sean Baylor, and you have to write about the ghosts of Monterey." Then it hit me why the hottest guy in our workshop was pretending interest in me instead of Vanessa, who'd made it beyond clear that she was available. "Is that why you asked me to have coffee with you? So that you could talk me into trading topics?"

"I'm not going to lie. It's one of the reasons. Not the only one, though."

"I can't do it, Jeremy." How could I explain to him how hard I'd fought to get this far, and how important it was for me to convince Henry Jaffa that I was worthy of mentoring? "I wish I could. I really do."

"So you're not going to trade with me?"

"I can't."

"Fine." He looked at me as if I were a stranger. "I'll do what I have to."

Then he turned and headed back toward the campus.

"You do that," I shouted to his back.

The wind swallowed my words, but I already felt better. And, yes, I felt worse, too.

NOTES TO SELF

Well, this day certainly sucks. First my mentor-to-be shuffles our topics. Now, I've gone from competing with Vanessa for Jeremy to competing with Jeremy for an article topic. I can still see his dismissive expression when he realized I wasn't going to trade with him, those veiled eyes. And I'm still betting that he's an Earth sign, probably that proud, Fixed Bull. I'll read up more after lunch with Candice. First, I just need to mull it all over. And right now, as much as I love being an Aquarius most of the time, I really hate that mulling-it-over aspect of my sign.

ARE YOU FIRE, EARTH, AIR, WATER?

By Logan McRae

Before you even attempt to guess someone's sign, you need to figure out the element. Yes, "What's your sign?" sounds way cooler than, "What's your element," but you need to start with the basics. Understanding your own element will also help you understand why you behave as you do. Each element has an up side and a down side, just as people do.

Fire

First, check out the body language. If someone is all over the place and trying to take charge—like the dreaded Vanessa—she is probably Fire. That means an Aries who wants to run everything but is often unable to be a finisher. A fiery Leo (like Nathan, my first and last boyfriend) wants to star in everything. A Sagittarius, with a mouth to rival Gemini's, is too busy running and talking and everything-elsing to know what he wants. Fire signs can be energetic, attractive, generous, and fun. The world would be dull without them.

Earth

Earth signs are all seeking stability. When they have it, the Taurus will relax, the Virgo will stop nitpicking, and the Capricorn will discover that there is more to life than work. Earth signs are comforting and consistent. These no-nonsense types can never be accused of having their heads in the clouds.

They can be slow to respond to a question or to render an opinion. But once that question is answered and the opinion rendered, you can bet it's forever.

Taurus is known for both persistence and a sense of fair play. Perfectionist Virgo tends to be critical of all including its Virgo-self. Hard-working Capricorns can be too serious for their own good.

Air

If someone is talking all of the time, you probably have an Air sign on your hands. Aquarius talks and spews the way the mad scientist does, to save the world. (I try to avoid that nasty aspect of my sign, but I plead guilty to my inability to settle on an immediate solution.)

Gemini talks to distribute information. Sometimes, that information sounds a whole lot like gossip. Don't blame Gemini. This sign lives to tell the truth—yours, mine, everyone else's. Regardless of how far a Gemini wanders from your life, this sign will always be curious about you. Libra talks to try to figure things out and present herself as balanced and positive. Although some Libras are critical and judgmental, not to mention narcissistic, basically, they are just Air signs trying to speak their piece.

With their creativity and honesty, Air signs add sparkle to life.

Water

In a word, emotional. In six words, tied to parents and the past. If the emotions are "Poor me," you just might have a Cancer on your hands. While Pisces pretends she isn't a victim, Cancer is happy to claim that title. Watery Scorpio is the one with the clenched, tight smile, the wonderful everything—until life punctures that perfect balloon with a pin of honesty.

Pisces takes up the rear of the zodiac and is sometimes treated like its doormat. If a Pisces is run over by a truck, even a truck he owns, driven by the guy he paid to drive it, the Pisces will say it's no big deal and retreat to his dream world.

The sometimes moody, always emotional Water signs are also some of the most caring in the zodiac. Even when their own lives are in turmoil, they are patient, loyal friends. Cancer would kill to protect a family member. Scorpio is beyond loyal. Pisces can put everyone else first. Even as stuck and mired as some Water signs are, they mean it when they say they care.

3

ALTHOUGH THE SUN SIGN IS NOT THE SUM, MANY OVERLOOK WHAT CAN BE LEARNED FROM THIS SIGN IN A RUSH TO ANALYZE MOON, MARS, VENUS, AND URANUS, AND ALL OF THE OTHER PLANETS. DO NOT HURRY THROUGH THE SUN. IT CAN REVEAL WHETHER SOMEONE IS FIXED, MUTABLE, CARDINAL, MASCU-LINE, OR FEMININE—ALL TERMS THAT YOU WILL LEARN ABOUT IN FUTURE CHAPTERS. FURTHERMORE, YOU'LL ALSO KNOW THE PLANETARY RULER OF EACH SIGN. SO, TAKE YOUR TIME, SLOW DOWN, AND ENJOY THIS LEISURELY JOURNEY THROUGH THE SUN.

—Fearless Astrology

*L*eisurely? Okay. Maybe I needed to go back and evaluate Jeremy a little more. After lunch, Candice went to the suite to study, and I walked aimlessly around the campus, wondering if I had done the right thing. There was no way I could have switched topics with Jeremy. And if I had? Just then, I realized that I was doing it again—the dreaded Aquarian batting it around in my brain. What I needed to do was take action. The library was right ahead of me. I didn't hesitate for a moment.

The guy at the desk was about my age with a streak of patent-leather red in his short, black hair.

"You're new, aren't you?" he asked. "How can I help you?"

"I'm with Writers Camp, and I'm looking for books on Monterey folk singers."

"Writers Camp?" Something shifted in his expression, and he seemed less open, more guarded. "Which singers?"

"Folkies from the sixties, anything with Sean Baylor in it."

"So, what's this? Sean Baylor Day? We have only a few books where he's mentioned. Five, actually."

"Great," I said.

"Not really." His look turned apologetic.

Then it hit me. "Let me guess. Someone just checked out those five books, right?"

He nodded. "Hey, he can't keep them longer than three weeks. Give me your contact information. If he returns them early, I'll let you know."

Even though I felt like crying, I reached for the pen he

offered and said, "Sure."

Students lingered outside, but Jeremy wasn't among them. He'd said he planned to study on the beach today—said he loved this place. If he meant it, I knew he'd be down there, as close as he could get to the ocean.

I went back to the library and asked the cute guy for directions. He told me it was about a two-mile hike to the beach, and I'd have to go through the army base and past abandoned buildings. The shorter route was under Highway 1 dunes and ice plant, but it would get me there.

Before I left, I couldn't help asking, "Are you an Aries or a Leo?"

He laughed and said, "Why?"

"Forget it. I'm just weird today."

"Astrology isn't weird. My girlfriend's really into it, and you are good."

"So?" I asked. "You are a Fire sign?"

"Aries all the way." He grinned. "*With* a Leo Moon."

I felt as if he'd given me a gift—a confirmation that I did know something about astrology. All I needed was enough information about Sean Baylor to write my article.

The walk through the ice plant-covered dunes was a little creepy. Totally isolated. No wonder so few students went to this part of the beach. I found Jeremy leaning against a boulder facing the sea. The books were scattered around him. One of them lay open in his lap, and he read from it into a recorder.

"Many who witnessed Baylor's dynamic performance at

the Monterey Pop Festival of 1967 agreed that he was destined for stardom. Yet, clues to his destructive personality had long been evident. The only question that remains is this one. Was his death an accident or suicide?"

"I believe you're supposed to be researching the ghosts of Monterey," I said.

Jeremy snapped off the recorder and looked up at me. "That's Candice's new topic. I got permission from Jaffa to write about Baylor, so don't be a poor loser."

"This isn't a contest," I said. "You took all five books. Can't you give me even a couple?"

"Why should I?"

"Because I can help you. I don't understand how you could deny me an opportunity to write my own take on Sean Baylor, especially since I'm willing to share it with you."

"What take is that? And please don't say astrology."

"Why don't you try it?" My cheeks blazed in the cold. "If you'll give me his birth date, I'll at least be able to suggest some basic traits."

"Enough," he asked, "to know if he was murdered or committed suicide?"

I stepped closer to him on the sand.

"I believe I can come closer than you can by just reading facts into a recorder."

He closed the book. "Well, I guess we disagree on that. I don't believe in astrology, but I want to be decent about this."

"Then, let me have one book, just one."

"It might be the one I need." He gave me that guarded smile of his. "Tell you what. Once I finish my article, you can have them all."

"Thanks a lot." My Aquarius mind battled with itself. There was only one thing to do.

He glanced at his book. "Then I guess I'll see you in class."

"If that's the way you want it." I reached down and snatched it out of his hands.

"Hey," he shouted. "Wait a minute."

But I was already running across the sand, clutching my prize.

NOTES TO SELF

Book thief. That's me. I have the stolen property, and I'm in bed now, studying the three photos of Sean Baylor in this collection. His eyes are so dark that they look like shadows. Unlike a lot of the singers from that time, he doesn't appear demonic, drugged, or pissed off. Maybe just lost. The quote Jeremy read into his recorder is on the front page of the Baylor section. There's little text within the book, and as I scan it, I realize there's no birth date for Baylor. Just my luck. The library failed me. Next stop, my mentor-to-be. He's certainly old enough to remember Sean Baylor. And he's already said he attended concerts here in the sixties. Time to take that run on the beach.

4

DO NOT WORRY, AQUARIUS, IF IT TAKES YOU SOME
TIME TO FIGURE OUT THE RIGHT DIRECTION OR THE
EASY ANSWER. LEAVE THE FLIPPANT RESPONSES AND
REACTIONS TO OTHER SIGNS. YOU REALLY DO HAVE ALL
OF THE DIRECTIONS AND MOST OF THE ANSWERS
WITHIN THAT INCREDIBLE BRAIN OF YOURS. GIVEN
TIME AND DISTANCE, YOU WILL FIND THE PATH THAT
YOU ARE SEEKING.

—*Fearless Astrology*

andice fired up the espresso machine early the
next morning. Noise and I don't mix well at 6 AM. I
lifted my head from the pillow and realized she'd
also turned on the television. Not a great combination.

"Sorry," she said. "Tatiyana is coming by along with Dirk, the hot guy with the British accent and the ponytail."

I remembered the voice but couldn't picture the hair. What was Dirk's topic? Oh, that's right. We no longer had our own topics.

"Who?" I asked.

"Dirk. He's hot."

"What about your boyfriend back home?"

"It's only coffee." Candice flipped a switch, and the machine roared like a garbage disposal.

"Want a cup?" she shouted over the racket.

"Sure."

I would have loved to stay in bed reading the *Fearless* section I'd started late last night. Instead, I showered, accepted Candice's tiny white cup, and watched the sun and the gray ocean. Then, I politely excused myself and headed down to the beach.

The cold air was like a sobering slap in the face, which was what I needed after the craziness of yesterday. I meant nothing to Jeremy. That was clear. So, now what I planned to do was conveniently run into Henry Jaffa and find out what he knew about Sean Baylor.

It didn't take long. Jaffa jogged along the beach in gray sweats. I waved. He walked over and joined me.

"You must be an early riser," he said.

"Not really. I'm just trying to avoid an espresso party in my room."

"Probably the same one I'm avoiding." He grinned.

"You were invited to my room?"

"Yes, if it's the one with the espresso machine," he said. "I know why I'm not there, but why aren't you?"

"Too much noise too early in the morning, I guess."

"Well put." He began to walk alongside me, huffing a little, but I was the one who could barely breathe. "By the way, I read your entrance essay. Although I know little about astrology, I'm intrigued."

"I was hoping to write more . . ." I didn't dare look at him and focused on the ocean instead. ". . . before we switched topics, I mean."

"So now you're writing about Sean Baylor," he said in that matter-of-fact way of his. "And I'll bet you're taking an astrological focus."

"Yes," I said, surprised that he'd guessed correctly a second time. "But I'm not sure. I mean, I don't know anything about Baylor. I can't get the right research material."

"And that's precisely the point. You understand that, don't you?"

"Not exactly," I admitted.

"Don't you see?" With the frizzy gray hair and the battered tennis shoes, he looked like anything but a famous writer. "Most of the students in the workshop objected to my changing their topics. You found a way to make it work. My compliments."

"Do you remember Baylor?" I asked.

"Of course." He spoke slowly, as if listening to something too far away for me to hear. "His voice could break your heart."

"What else can you tell me about him?"

"Nothing."

His voice was so soft, so kind, that I wondered if I'd heard him correctly. "Nothing at all?" I asked.

"That's your job," he said. "See you later."

My compliments.

What had I done to earn that? And did I really have Henry Jaffa on my side?

I walked into class early, hoping that I did.

Not early enough. Vanessa was parked in the front row again, her black hair fluffed around bare shoulders. Oh, that was cool. Showing flesh—not to mention cleavage—before 9 AM.

"Hey, Logan." She gave me a windshield-wiper wave. "I was hoping you'd be here."

"You were?"

"Sure. I stopped by for espresso in your room. I even invited Henry. He's been mentoring me, I guess you could say."

"Oh really? I'm sorry I missed him."

It was a test. Would she admit Jaffa hadn't been there or try to make me believe he had?

"No problem. I'm just really glad you're here."

Since when?

"Why's that?" I asked.

"Because of the Sean Baylor connection. Haven't you heard?"

"Heard what?"

"Baylor's ghost. People at Stokes Restaurant have heard him singing. I knew it the first night we went there. I sensed his spirit."

"Don't start that with me," I told her. "You wouldn't know *spirit* if it . . ."

"No, she's right. I heard it on the news this morning." Jeremy stepped inside, not looking at me, staring only at her.

Henry Jaffa followed. "I heard that story too," he said.

"So did I." Candice was right behind him. "It came on the TV news a few minutes after you left, Logan."

Tatiyana and the British guy arrived next. Within a few moments, they were all gathered around Vanessa.

"Can you believe it?" she gushed. "I heard that the *Ghost Seekers* series might be filming an episode here."

Then she gave me a nasty smirk.

If she hadn't done that, if she'd just smiled, I might have remained silent. If she'd acted just a little less bitchy.

"I won't believe it until I see it." I glared right back at her.

"Excellent idea." Jaffa walked up to me. "Perhaps we need a field trip. Let's wait, though, until some of these rumors are confirmed. I have a writing exercise for you this morning."

"What confirmation could you want?" Vanessa demanded.

"The type that takes place over time. I have no intention of canceling class to go running to a restaurant I've already visited. Now, please take your seats so we can get started."

"I'd say a ghost is pretty important." Vanessa remained

standing, her anger still focused on me. "Just because Logan doesn't believe it, doesn't mean it doesn't exist."

"If your ghost is there now, he'll be there later," I said. "What's the matter, Vanessa? Did the dog eat your homework again?"

"There's only one dog in this room . . ."

"Enough," Jaffa said.

"But you, of all people, should want to check this out." Vanessa shot to the front of the class. "Let's take a vote. How many want to leave and go to the restaurant?"

Hands shot up. The British guy, Tatiyana, even Candice, my own roommate, betraying me. Jeremy crossed his arms and stared at me.

"Anybody who leaves this room leaves it for good," Jaffa said quietly. "This is not a democracy. It's my classroom, and we are doing a writing exercise, period."

NOTES TO SELF

As my gram would say, Jaffa socked it to them. Watching him in action was pretty cool. Mr. Franklin, my English teacher back home, is loud and explosive. Henry Jaffa, as calm and borderline dorky as he may seem, can freeze a classroom into silence by a slight change in his tone. After he had made it clear that no one would leave the room to go rushing to a ghost site, Vanessa marched to the end of the table and sat next to Jeremy. It must have been a first for that Fire sign to sit in back.

Jaffa asked us to do something he called the ten-thousand-word sentence. That's right—five minutes to write about our greatest passions—with no punctuation. It was supposed to help us find our voice by removing our focus on grammar, punctuation, and criticism. I glanced down at Jeremy, who wrote only a couple of words on the page as Vanessa scrawled happily beside him. I could only imagine her passions, but what about mine? I think that I did as much crossing-out as I did writing.

THE 10,000-WORD SENTENCE

By Logan McRae

Since I discovered astrology I have become passionate about using it as a ~~guide~~ tool to understanding myself and others and I know that being an Aquarius I am always sometimes slow to come to conclusions as I was earlier this year when I trusted the wrong person and always want to ~~overthink~~ analyze every situation except that right now the situation is so important that I need a game plan and now because the topic I'm supposed to write about isn't a topic I ~~care~~ know about and because ~~a certain guy~~ some people don't want me to write about the topic I have to remember ~~my dream~~ what is important and know that even if it takes an Aquarian longer to come up with a game plan it is the right game plan or at least we Fixed signs will think it is and I guess the real reason I'm writing about this is ~~I'm scared~~ I am concerned about how to combine my writing ability with everything I've learned about astrology and everything I hope to learn about this ~~obscure~~ folk singer Sean Baylor so that I write an article ~~that can be published~~ that is worthy of merit and for that reason I am feeling ~~like a fish out of water as my gram would say~~ a little anxious about what steps to take next and as I said I guess the reason I'm writing this right now is that I am really ~~terrified~~ concerned.

5

Dealing with an Aries can feel a little like playing with Fire. Which is exactly what you're doing. You can't win, but you might be able to negotiate, if you can lower the heat, that is. You need to figure out which Aries is standing in your way. Is it the running-down-the-street-naked Aries? Or is it someone more reasonable and focused? Treat your average Aries as you would a child. That means that you have to be the adult.

—*Fearless Astrology*

anessa was an Aries. I should have guessed it, but with all the dramatics and center-staging, I had almost decided on Leo. At least I got the Fire part right. When I asked her sign, she proudly announced her birth date. April freakin' first. April Fool's Day, for sure. If she showed up naked at Jaffa's reading and beach party tonight, it wouldn't surprise me.

Not that I cared. My only focus now was learning Sean Baylor's sign, and I could find it in one of those books I *hadn't* stolen from Jeremy. I only hoped he would show up. As unpredictable as he was, there was no telling.

The local news stations were going nuts over the Baylor ghost and the fact that the *Ghost Seekers* television show was sending representatives to check it out. If the media drew attention to Baylor and started digging into his history, that could be good for me, and I might not need Jeremy's books at all. I couldn't take any chances, though.

Our class met on the beach early that evening. It was cold, with a sharp wind blowing in from the ocean. Vanessa was the only one flashing flesh. I was really starting to dislike this girl. And, yes, it angered me just a little that she, in her acid-green sweater, was giggling and sharing a plate of food with Candice, who the last time I checked, was supposed to be my roommate.

Jeremy stood talking to Jaffa, both of them facing the ocean, their backs to the rest of us. This was the first time I'd seen them exchange more than a few words, but that wouldn't hurt my chances with Jaffa. Jeremy had made it clear that he wasn't looking for a writing mentor. All I had to do was convince him to trade books with me.

Most of the students sat at one of two long redwood tables. Platters of grilled tri-tip steak were lined along the other one. I got in the food line behind Tati, as she had asked me to call her. Wearing a violet tunic that matched the streak in her hair, she seemed pleased that she was being chatted up by Dirk, the hot British guy. The espresso party must have gone well, for her, at least.

I put two slices of tri-tip on a paper plate, along with a warm sourdough roll.

"Don't you want some mustard?"

I turned and looked up into Jeremy's face. How had he gotten over here so fast? This was not the time to tell him— not that I ever would—that mustard made my nose turn red.

"I'm fine, thanks."

As I spoke, a very bundled Henry Jaffa made his way to a microphone at the end of the table and began shuffling through papers.

"You can tell he's not from California," Jeremy said. "He doesn't know how to dress for the beach."

I could feel him edging toward something, the way he had when he'd invited me to coffee and then tried to get me to switch topics. His cute-boy con job had worked on me once, and I guessed he was going to try it again.

Vanessa left Candice and bounced up to the front, as if she

were Jaffa's personal assistant. Jeremy watched her a little longer than necessary. That gave me the courage to ignore my passive Pisces Moon and say what was on my mind.

"Let me guess," I told him. "You're talking to me right now only because you're hoping that you can get me to turn over a certain book. Isn't that right?"

He nodded as if impressed that I had figured out that this cozy conversation of ours had nothing to do with any interest he might have in me. "A certain book of *mine*."

"It belongs to the school library. You just checked it out."

"Which makes it mine for the whole three weeks. Play fair, Logan. It has photos in it, and the ones you didn't steal don't have a single one."

That was news to me.

"It does have three photos in it," I said, "but I'm writing from an astrological perspective. I need a birth date."

"If I give it to you, you'll use it for your own paper."

"So what? Why do you care what I do? If you want to write your piece on Sean Baylor, go for it. If yours is the one that gets published, I'm all right with that, too."

"Do you mean it?" He looked surprised.

"Of course I do. I don't care if I'm published tomorrow or next year. And I can see that we both have very different goals." I set my untouched paper plate on the table and looked into those amazing eyes. "I have the book with the photos, Jeremy. You have the ones with the information I need. Why can't we share?"

"Because I can't . . ."

"Can't what?"

"I don't know."

"Well, when you figure it out, I hope you'll agree that I'm not asking all that much."

Just then, a bald guy and a girl with long, blond hair walked across the beach with the friendly Aries librarian I had met earlier.

"This is a private gathering," Jaffa said in that soft but crystal-clear voice of his. "A class meeting."

"I know that, Mr. Jaffa," the librarian replied. "These folks are from *Ghost Seekers*. I told him that some of you people have an interest in Sean Baylor, and they'd like to talk to anyone who thinks they've seen his ghost."

"I have!" Vanessa rushed up to them. The Aries freak show was now picturing herself on TV.

"You actually *saw* him?" I asked.

"I sensed his spirit the first night. I told you that."

The blond girl was tall with a sprayed-on tan and a dazzling smile. "Other people have reported similar experiences. I'm Emily, and this is Doug. Come on with us to Stokes Restaurant. Were going to talk to everyone who saw or heard anything to be sure there's sufficient evidence to do a segment."

"I'll be there," Vanessa said.

"I'm coming too." Jaffa walked over to them. In the fading light, his usually calm expression looked eager and childlike. "We'll have to postpone the reading."

"Finally," Vanessa said. "I kept telling you people that we should check out Stokes again."

He ignored her comment and addressed the rest of us. "Let's all go. At least, we'll find out how a national television show on the paranormal searches for material."

I followed the others across the beach, aware of Jeremy beside me.

"Are you going?" he asked.

"Sure. I'm interested in seeing what they do. Besides, Jaffa told us to be there."

"But you haven't eaten."

"I'll get something later."

"I haven't eaten much myself. There's a pizza place next to the restaurant."

This guy had tried to use me twice to get information on the topic he wanted to write about. I was not going to take the pizza bait he was dangling.

"So what about the books?" I asked.

He grinned in that fake/charming way I'd already learned to read through. "If I tell you Sean Baylor's birth date, will you promise to give me the book with the pictures?"

"Sure," I said. "If you give me another one in return."

"You don't back down, do you?"

"It's not a matter of backing down," I said. "It's a matter of doing what's right."

"You don't understand, Logan. I have to get published in that anthology."

"That doesn't make you my enemy. The anthology is a fine goal, but it's not my ultimate goal."

"Then, what is? What could matter more than the anthology?"

I wanted to tell him that all I really hoped for was Henry Jaffa as a mentor. But I couldn't speak the words. I was afraid he'd laugh, or worse, that he'd pity me for even daring to hope.

"It's personal," I said, and then realized how harsh and snippy that sounded. "What I mean is . . ."

"Tell me." His voice was suddenly gentle.

"Let's just say that you and I are not in competition for anything important." I started to walk away, but he reached out for my arm and pulled me next to him.

"June fifth." His breath in my ear was so warm that I shivered.

"What?"

"June fifth. That's when Sean Baylor was born."

A Gemini. I took a step back. "Thank you for that. At least, it's a beginning."

He smiled and said, "I like beginnings."

"So you will give me the book?"

"I promised, and so did you. I'll bring it to class tomorrow."

"You will?"

"Hey, I'm on my way to a ghost-stalking session. I might as well check out what you can do with astrology while I'm at it."

In spite of his friendly manner, I knew he was making fun of me.

"Well," I told him, "maybe you'll be surprised."

"I hope so," he said. "I like surprises, too."

NOTES TO SELF

Unfortunately for Vanessa, she was unable to connect with Sean Baylor's spirit at Stokes tonight. Neither was anyone else. Jaffa went all Sherlock Holmes on us, questioning the staff and taking rapid notes. Emily and Doug, the *Ghost Seekers* researchers, were clearly disappointed. They kept ordering wine as if hoping the female ghost upstairs would suddenly appear and sprinkle salt in their glasses. After the second or third round, Emily stage-whispered to Doug that they ought to leave right then. He whispered back something about their agreement with the network. Then, the two of them settled at the bar to argue about it, and Jaffa told us it was time to go. Jeremy was the first one out the door.

I feel like a kid who just ran from the classroom into recess. Right now, Candice is outside making the nightly call to her guy back home, and I can finally dig into *Fearless Astrology* one more time. So, Sean Baylor was a Gemini, was he? So is Chili, one of my two best friends. Because of her, I'm already aware of all of the great-communicator, fickle-love stuff about Gemini. You're next, Baylor. And I meant what I said to Jeremy tonight. If he can write a better paper than I can, that's okay, too. What I didn't say was that I intend to do everything possible to make sure that doesn't happen.

6

Her chart was both the perfect astrological recipe for success in the entertainment business and a cocktail for personal tragedy. In spite of her tremendous talent, she was lost in her search for direction, and perhaps, the strong partner she believed would protect her. So, can a Gemini succeed as an actor, singer, politician, or leader? Many have. If this is your path in life, tread carefully and think before you speak, act, or, most of all, before you fall in love.

—Fearless Astrology

hy I was I spending my time reading about a star who had died in 1962? Because back when my gram wrote *Fearless Astrology*, Helen Hunt, Angelina Jolie, Nicole Kidman, Brooke Shields, Alanis Morissette, and a whole bunch of other Geminis had yet to be born. The most famous Gem entertainer back then, according to *Fearless*, was Marilyn Monroe, whom my gram called the quintessential Gemini star. Not to mention her Leo Rising (Fire and a need to be on stage) and Aquarian Moon (Air and a need to give to the world).

Reading about her gave me a hint about how Sean Baylor—even though he didn't live long enough to achieve the great success predicted for him—might have been back in the sixties. A strong communicator. Probably not too stable in his love life. I needed more information about him. Moon, Venus, Mars. But at least I had a starting place. I tried not to think about Jeremy's expression when he had said he *liked* beginnings. Tried not to think about him at all, although I'd thought about little else since last night. Before class started today, I was going to visit the local newspaper office and do some Baylor tracking of my own. All I needed was a helpful computer geek in the editorial department.

The *Coastal Times* building was smaller than I had expected with large tinted glass windows. There had to be someone working in there. I went to the front door and knocked. No response. I knocked harder. Still nothing. Harder still. Then I rattled the handle, perhaps with little more exuberance than was necessary.

All off a sudden, an alarm began shrieking. I looked around, feeling like a car thief caught in the act. Just then, a short, shades-wearing security guard appeared out of nowhere.

"Stay where you are." Although only about a foot taller than I, he was built like a wrestler. And he was wearing enough scent for three guys.

"Hey," I yelled over the noise, "I'm not armed and not trying to break in."

"Then what are you doing messing around here? Vandals hit us two times last week." He maintained his military stance and tapped a code into the keypad on the door. The alarm went silent.

"I'm not a vandal," I said.

"So you were just trying to bust through a locked door?"

"I figured you'd already be open."

"Only the classified office," he said.

"Not Editorial?"

"Absolutely not. Those folks upstairs don't want to be disturbed."

"If the door's locked, how do you expect anyone to get to classified?"

"Before this interruption, I was just getting around to opening it," he said, and I got another whiff of the spicy citrus scent he had applied with a heavy hand. "And, yeah, I know the alarm's tricky when someone messes with the handle. You're not the first one to set it off."

"So, can I go inside?"

"Sure, if you're looking for classified."

"I am," I lied and tried to think fast. "I want to run a high school graduation announcement." Premature by about two years, but he didn't have to know that.

"Go on inside, then. Helen at the front desk will help you."

He jingled the keys again, and there I was, heading inside the glass door without any idea of where to go next.

A gray-haired woman at the front desk was busy with a call, so I just smiled and walked past her.

"Wait." She waved at me to stop.

"It's okay, Helen," I said. "I talked to the guard. He said I could come in."

Then I headed down the hall and stopped abruptly at a corridor covered by greenish carpeting that might have been new about the time I was born. The sign on the wall pointed left and read, "Advertising," which no doubt included classified advertising. The one to the right read, "Circulation." Beyond it was the back guard station. Between those two destinations, in an alcove, was an elevator with a red enamel door.

I stared at it for a moment and then recalled the guard's words. "Those folks upstairs don't want to be disturbed."

I walked over and stepped inside a compartment that was big enough for me and maybe one and a half of my closest friends. The little cage rattled up to the top floor, and I stepped out into a large area next to a counter with two coffeepots. Several feet ahead of me, surrounded by windows overlooking Monterey, were maybe a half dozen or more people intent on the computer screens before them. The newsroom. I had found it.

"This is not the way to classified."

I turned, and there was guard man again, looking not at all pleased.

"Where'd you come from?" I asked.

"I took the stairs. Now, tell me the truth this time. You're too young to be running a high school graduation announcement. You don't look like a runaway, vandal, or druggie, so I'm going to give you one more chance before I decide whether to kick you out of here or call the cops."

He took off the shades, and I saw his eyes for the first time. They were dark, deep brown, and kind enough that I decided to tell him the truth. Part of it, at least.

"I'm in a summer workshop at the college, and I really, really need some information right away. This is the only time I could come."

"Why didn't you just tell me that in the first place?"

"Because you wouldn't have let me in, would you?"

"That's not the point." He tried to appear all stern and official. Had to be another Earth sign. Just what I needed. "What kind of information are you looking for anyway?"

"Any and everything I can find out about Sean Baylor, a folk singer who used to live here."

He stepped back. "The one they're saying is dead?"

"Dead and haunting the restaurant downtown," I told

him. "Someone around here must remember what happened when he died. There have got to be articles about him in your archives."

"I wouldn't know anything about that."

"But you must know who can. Please help me."

"Right now, you need to leave and come back during business hours." He pushed the elevator button. "My boss will be here any minute, and I do things by the book."

"Virgo?" I asked before I could stop myself.

"What?"

"I mean, isn't there someone around here who knows anything about Sean Baylor?"

"Maybe." He stared at the closing door and hit the button again. "You'd probably ought to talk to Mercedes."

"Who's that?"

"Mercedes Lloyd-Chambers, editorial librarian. Sometimes she comes in early." He started toward an office to the right of the elevator. "Mercedes is cool, but don't tell anyone else that I let you in."

"If it's so against your rules, why'd you do it?"

The look he gave me was so incredibly sad that I wished I hadn't asked. "Nothing you'd understand. Do you think it's true what they're saying? About Baylor's ghost being in that restaurant?"

We stopped outside the door to the editorial library.

"I don't know. There are people who think so, and a lot of fakes who will claim to have seen him. Why do you care?"

"Not because of me. Because of someone I lost. If Baylor's ghost is still here, maybe that person is here too."

"Who?"

"Never mind." He shifted into security guard mode again. "Let's see if Mercedes is in." He knocked on the door. No one opened it. "Sorry," he said.

"Can I leave my phone number for her?"

"Sure," he said. "Write it down and give it to Helen at the front desk."

We rode the tiny elevator back to the ground floor. At least I had a name. Mercedes Lloyd-Chambers.

"Thank you for trying to help me," I told him at the door. "And I'm really sorry that I set off your alarm."

"Like I said, it's real touchy. Besides, it goes with the territory. The other guy did the same thing."

I stopped on the carpeted hall and fought to keep the tone of my voice relatively sane. "What other guy?"

"A kid from your school, I think. He was in yesterday morning. Set off the alarm the same as you did." He smiled as if unaware that my heartbeat was suddenly out of control.

"He did?"

"About the same time as you did it. He was looking for information about Sean Baylor too."

My mind was on fire, blazing from one fact to another. Jeremy had been here yesterday and then had the nerve to flirt with me at the beach party. We had agreed to exchange books. All the time, he'd been one step ahead of me, caring only about his own paper, his obsession with Sean Baylor, and his music.

"Who'd he talk to?" I asked.

"No one." He grinned. "You got farther than he did."

"Good." I reached out my hand. "I'm Logan."

He shook it and said, "Richard."

"Would you ask Mercedes to call me? I need to talk to her."

"That other kid, he left his number too. You two aren't working together, are you?"

"No." I owed him this much of the truth. "Let me give you my cell."

I retrieved a piece of paper from my bag, and printed my number on it, along with: MERCEDES, PLEASE CALL ME. I NEED INFORMATION ABOUT SEAN BAYLOR.

"Thanks," I told the guard. "If you have any influence, please ask her to call me first, okay?"

"I guess I could try," he said. "But my boss is due any minute right now. You'd better haul."

NOTES TO SELF

I hauled. Richard, my new friend, has already helped me more than he can ever imagine. Maybe Mercedes will call me. If not, I'll contact her. At least, Jeremy doesn't know about her. He may have beaten me here, but I beat him to the source. And, yes, I can't wait to see him in class and mention my visit to the newspaper. I'm in the backseat of a taxi that's been metering me longer than I'd planned. I hope my Virgo dad can understand that effect on my allowance. I'm going to be late to class, but it's worth it. Now I know that, no matter how friendly Jeremy acts, he sees me only as competition. Maybe even the enemy. Next goal—figure out his sign—starting with immovable Earth.

A REMINDER ABOUT EARTH SIGNS. THEY ARE NOT ALL
STATIC, STUBBORN PEOPLE, WHO REFUSE TO CHANGE.
YES, THOSE TAURUS, VIRGO, AND CAPRICORNS ARE
LIKE BOATS THAT ARE HAPPIEST CLOSE TO PORT. BUT
WHEN THEY VENTURE AWAY FROM HOME AS MANY
EARTH SIGNS DARE TO DO, THEY MOVE FORWARD WITH
CONFIDENCE. DON'T EVER WORRY ABOUT THE PACE OF
AN EARTH SIGN. IT MAY ARRIVE BEHIND THE BLAZING,
SELF-INVOLVED FIRE SIGNS, THE NONSTOP TALKING
AIR SIGNS, AND THE LONG SUFFERING WATER-MARTYR
SIGNS. BUT IT WILL GET THERE. AND WHEN THAT
EARTH SIGN ARRIVES, IT WILL MAKE ITSELF KNOWN,
AND ONLY THEN, DROP THE ANCHOR.

—Fearless Astrology

arth signs. Yes, I was certain Jeremy was one. And now that I thought about it, maybe others in this group. Candice, for sure. And Tati, with that perfect hair? Maybe her, too. Was it possible that I was surrounded by Earth signs? Was that why I felt so overwhelmed? Was my Air being smothered by too much Earth?

I didn't know what sign the cab driver was—something passive-aggressive, for sure. He stopped at every yellow light and seemed to be taking the longest route to the college. I began to get nervous.

Jaffa had been known to kick out students who didn't show up on time. He was also supposed to have flushed someone's cell phone down a toilet, but that had to be an urban myth. I was going to be late, and not just five or ten minutes. More like twenty or thirty.

Finally, the driver pulled up in front of the college. I shoved some bills at him, jumped out, and ran the rest of the way into the classroom.

Dirk was the first one I spotted. His ponytail, that is. He sat, with his back facing the door, in the front row between Tati and Candice.

Jaffa stood at the podium, reading from *Love and Murder*. When I came in, he stopped. Most of the kids turned to stare at me. All but Jeremy, in the back row, who was focused on Jaffa. Or pretending to be.

"Good morning, Logan," Jaffa said. "I'm pleased that you could join us."

As soft as his voice was, I sensed major irritation.

"I'm really sorry." I made a point to look at Jeremy, who was making a point not to look at me. "I was doing some research at the newspaper office, and I had to take a taxi back here."

Jeremy tensed in his chair, and I knew I'd managed to surprise him. At the moment, though, that was a minor victory.

"Henry." Vanessa shot her hand up in that irritating way of hers. "Does that mean it's all right for us to take off from class if we're doing research and can't find a taxi to get us back in time?"

He shook his head. "Absolutely not. As I'm sure you've all heard, I have little tolerance for tardiness, cell phones, or people who cut class. But not to the degree that has been exaggerated by some of my former students."

"I didn't know I was going to be this late," I told him. "You said it was my job to find out about Sean Baylor. I thought I'd have enough time to visit the newspaper and get here, but I ran into some problems."

"What kind of problems? And, please, take a seat, Logan. Perhaps you'd care to share what you found out this morning."

"Sure." My voice sounded scratchy, but I forced myself to walk to the front and sit down next to Candice. "Well, I started by talking to a security guard at the newspaper about Sean Baylor." I turned and smiled into Jeremy's face. "The same guard you talked to yesterday, Jeremy."

"And that made you late?" His doubtful attitude was pure

Earth. "No one could make it past the front door at that place."

"I did," I said.

"You did?"

"Made it past the front door, into the editorial department." It was all I could do to stop short of mentioning Mercedes.

"No way."

"And what did you learn?" Jaffa said.

"That there is a possible source who might have known Sean Baylor. A source the guard believes might talk to me."

"Who?" Jeremy asked.

"Who cares?" Vanessa said. "Baylor's spirit is at the restaurant. We don't need a source to connect with him. Too bad you missed most of Henry's reading, Logan. It was awesome."

I glanced at the book on Jaffa's podium and asked, "Was it the section about the man and woman in Santa Fe who were so convinced they were past-life lovers that they both murdered their current spouses?"

"This book published only last month," Jaffa said. "When did you read it?"

"A couple of weeks ago. I hope you'll tell us how you researched the guy who poisoned all three of his wives." That should shut up Vanessa Aries Mouth for a minute.

"You *have* read it," Jaffa said.

"Your other books too. I'm really sorry I was late."

"Logan, you have a source, and that is the beginning." Jaffa's eyes gleamed. "Tell me, class. Should she have come here or have gone there? If you are serious about writing, these are the questions you need to ask yourself."

"I think she should have gone," Tati said. "Because she got results, and results are all that matter."

"I agree with Tati." Dirk said in his cute accent. "Logan is familiar with your books, and you can tell how much she wanted to be at this reading. Yet, she put her own work first."

The rest of the class murmured agreement. Except for Jeremy, that is, who looked out the window, and Vanessa, who glared at me.

"Well done, Logan." Jaffa seemed to regard me with new respect. "You've helped me prove the point I wanted to make to all of you today. Break the rules when the end justifies the means. Put your story first. Who else in this room, other than Logan, put your story first today?"

A nervous silence filled the room.

Next to me, Candice slowly lifted her hand. "I did research last night," she said.

"Me, too." Tati raised her hand, as well.

"Yeah," Dirk said. "I did a little work myself."

Nothing from Vanessa. Nothing from Jeremy.

"Tell her, Henry," Vanessa piped up in that nervous squeak of hers. "Tell her about the ghost-seeking session."

"Vanessa is referring to our field trip." Jaffa's sigh sounded a little annoyed. "We are planning to visit Stokes tonight before the TV people leave. It's mandatory that everyone in class attends. And now, if it's all right with you folks, I'd like to finish my reading."

"Finally," Vanessa muttered. "I was starting to wonder if . . ."

An irritating chiming from my backpack interrupted her.

"Whose phone is that?" Jaffa demanded.

"Mine. I'm so sorry." I ripped open my pack tried to find it. "I don't know how . . ."

"Well, turn it off."

I didn't know what to do.

Finally, the chiming stopped. I found the phone and lifted it from my bag. The caller ID was still lit, and I stared at the name still showing there.

MercLC.

Make that Mercedes Lloyd-Chambers.

Still clutching the phone in my hand, I looked into Henry Jaffa's eyes. "It's my source," I said. "The one from the newspaper."

NOTES TO SELF

Back there in the classroom, I had what my gram would call a moment of mini-redemption. I'd come off like an absolute flake, but then that phone call from a legitimate source kind of made everything okay. Until I tried to call her back, that is. Mercedes had not answered her phone. It just rang and rang as I just looked stupid and more stupid. At least, Jaffa didn't flush my cell phone down the toilet. Instead, he began reading again. The man is amazing. I can't wait to see what he does at the restaurant tonight. In the meantime, I need to get away from all the drama and try to digest a large helping of *Fearless Astrology*.

8

CARDINAL. FIXED. MUTABLE. EACH OF THESE IS A QUALITY, AND EVERY SUN SIGN HAS ONE. DOMINANT SIGNS ARE CARDINAL, CONSISTENT SIGNS ARE FIXED, AND FLEXIBLE SIGNS ARE MUTABLE. THIS IS JUST SHORTHAND FOR EXPLAINING WHICH SUN SIGNS ARE MORE LIKELY TO TAKE CHARGE, HANG ON, OR QUICKLY ADAPT TO CHANGE. ARE YOU DEALING WITH ARIES, LIBRA, CANCER, OR CAPRICORN? WELCOME TO THE LAND OF THE CARDINAL QUALITY. THESE PEOPLE WANT TO TAKE CHARGE AND WILL DEFINITELY TRY TO. THE FIXED SIGNS OF TAURUS, LEO, SCORPIO, AND AQUARIUS ARE SLOWER TO MOVE AND DON'T LIKE TO

BE WRONG, EVEN WHEN THEY ARE. MUTABLE GEMINI, VIRGO, SAGITTARIUS, AND PISCES DEAL WITH CHANGE IN MANY WAYS THAT VARY FROM EMBRACING IT TO IGNORING IT. BUT ALL OF THEM HANDLE IT. SO, DON'T JUST LOOK AT THE SUN SIGN. LOOK ALSO AT THE QUALITY OF THAT SIGN.

—*Fearless Astrology*

I already knew that I was a Fixed sign, and I didn't need *Fearless* to tell me that. Now, I realized that Henry Jaffa and Jeremy were Fixed too. And Vanessa, of course, was Cardinal, so she had not only the me-me-me of Aries, but the mistaken idea that she was a leader. Tonight should be fun.

Candice had dared me to guess her sign that morning, and was shocked when I said, "Virgo." She wasn't a detail freak like my dad, but she did like everything in its place. And she had that calm, serene personality.

As I had hoped, Jaffa was on the bus. And, of course, Jeremy was not. Neither were Candice, Dirk, nor the dreaded Vanessa. Since Dirk was the only one with a car, the four of them were probably riding together. If that were the case, I didn't blame Candice. In spite of her boyfriend back in Colorado, I could sense that she liked Dirk. As for Jeremy and Vanessa—they deserved each other.

Although I was hoping to sit by Jaffa, he was in the back, dressed for a snowstorm, as usual, and scribbling in a notebook. Only the boldest of Fire signs would have dared to distract him. Just then, Tati waved at me, and I took the seat beside her. She seemed a little quiet, and I wondered if it was because Dirk was clearly elsewhere.

The bus parked beside the restaurant, and we got off.

"Logan, wait." I turned, and there was Jaffa, that thick wool navy scarf flying behind him as he caught up with me. "I want to hear about your source," he said. "The reporter at the newspaper. What did she have to say about Sean Baylor?"

"We haven't spoken yet, but I left several voice mails. She's worked at the newspaper a long time. The guard told me she probably knows about Baylor."

"Back then, the performers at the pop festival were completely accessible to the press. If your source was working at that time, she may well have interviewed him."

I felt a chill and knew he was right. Mercedes might actually have spoken with Baylor.

Just then, a group of four swept in front of us: Candice and Dirk, Vanessa and Jeremy. All of them were laughing and talking. The Aries wore another of what must have been an endless assortment of plunging tops. This one was black velvet, and there was enough going on above and below that deep neckline to keep Jeremy interested. Candice and Dirk were far less blatant, both in the way they dressed and the distance they kept between them.

"Hey, Logan." Vanessa was immediately in my face. "Candice said that you guessed her sign. How'd you pull off that little trick?"

Thanks, roommate. "No trick. I figured it out the same way I figured out that you're an Aries."

"Well, that had to be a major no-brainer. All you did was ask my birthday."

Jeremy chuckled, and I fought the urge to shoot him a nasty look.

"Vanessa," I said, "you are textbook Aries. I only asked your birthday to confirm what I had already guessed."

"Textbook? What's that supposed to mean?" She took a quick look back at Jeremy and heaved such a heavy sigh that I probably wasn't the only one wondering if she'd stay inside that top. "Since I'm stuck with writing that boring astrology paper, you could at least tell me where to find out more about Aries."

"The other eleven are pretty interesting too," I said.

"Eleven what?"

Eleven freaking signs! Isn't that what we're talking about?

Before I could translate that initial reaction into an unemotional Aquarius response, I realized that Jaffa had moved closer.

"Were you really able to guess her Sun sign by just observing her?" He peered at me intently, and I no longer cared whether or not Vanessa thought I was a fake.

"Appearance is part of it," I told him, "but behavior is a major factor. Aries can be one of the easiest to identify because so many of them have, well, I guess you could say an intense interest in themselves."

"What a crock," Vanessa snapped.

"Really?" Jaffa asked, as if he hadn't heard her.

"Oh, yes. In some books, they're referred to as the babies of the Zodiac, although some of them are extremely evolved." I shrugged as if to say that no Aries in this group necessarily qualified for that designation. "They're also Cardinal signs. Not Fixed, the way you and I are."

"We're the same sign?" he asked.

"Yes, we are. Fixed and Air, which means that in spite of all our great intentions, we Aquarians can get stuck trying to figure out which intention is the most important at any given moment. I know I do."

"So do I. And you figured out my sign, how? Just by evaluating my appearance and behavior?"

"No." I smiled into that squinty-eyed face of his. "*Your* birth date is all over the Internet. I looked it up my first night here."

He laughed. "I figured as much, and I'm impressed by your honesty."

"I wouldn't lie about looking up someone's sign," I said.

Vanessa giggled and whispered something to Jeremy.

Jaffa didn't seem to notice. "The zodiac is fascinating, isn't it?" he said. "Once I finish this book, I am going to spend some time researching astrology. Perhaps you . . ."

Just then, the door opened, and in walked Emily and Doug, the *Ghost Seekers* researchers. Behind them was a bald older guy carrying a camera.

"Hi, kids," Emily said. "Thanks for joining us." She seemed more positive than she had the night before. "Even though we haven't been able to document anything, there have been several reports of activity, so we're giving it one last shot."

"I knew it," Vanessa said, and squeezed Jeremy's arm.

He looked pretty unhappy. I started to feel sorry for him and then told myself that no one had forced him to come here with Vanessa.

"Let's get started," the camera guy said. "Where to, Emily?"

"Up there."

She walked up the narrow staircase, with Doug, the camera guy, and Jaffa right behind them. I stood below with Tati and the others.

"What are we supposed to be doing?" I asked.

"I'm not sure," Tati said.

"Go looking," Vanessa said. "The ghost is Sean Baylor's. I told you that I sensed him the first night, but you wouldn't listen."

"Of course, I did." I forced myself to smile. "It is pretty difficult not to listen when *you* speak."

She pondered that one a moment and whispered something else to Jeremy. He shook his head and moved away from her toward the stairs.

"I was just telling him that he was right about a certain person exaggerating her abilities," Vanessa said.

"Really?" Any snotty comment I shot back would only make it look as if she and I were in competition for him. Instead, I pretended I didn't understand. "Well, let's see what we can uncover."

We began to explore the place, spreading out but still keeping in the general direction of the TV crew. The top floor of the restaurant was dimly lit. Even so, I could tell that it had once been part of an elegant mansion. With its chilled air and maze of rooms, it seemed as if it belonged to the past. The more we explored, the colder it seemed to become.

Jaffa disappeared into one of the rooms lining the hall. I reminded myself that I had never seen a ghost, and from what I'd read in Jaffa's books, there was no reason to fear them anyway. Still, it didn't feel all that friendly up here, almost as if I was disturbing a place that didn't want me in it. If there were any spirits hanging around, they were probably trapped by some force I couldn't begin to imagine. Maybe by their own unfinished business. They couldn't just walk back down the stairs the way I was going to do right now.

The stairs were no longer where I had thought they were. Somehow, I'd gotten turned around. No reason to panic, though. One scream out of me, and the TV people would be here in seconds.

To my right, I could hear what sounded like muted voices. They seemed to be coming from a room across the hall. Maybe the TV people were in there. Or maybe someone, *something* else. Ghosts didn't hurt people. Only other people did.

Still, it was dark, and I was lost in a place that was supposed to be haunted.

Just as I started to turn away, I heard the high pitch of someone's laughter. No ghost ever sounded like that.

I reached for the knob and yanked open the door.

Nothing. Only darkness. Then I heard something. A whisper, then silence.

I felt for the switch and flipped it.

There they were, Vanessa and Jeremy, standing close. Very close.

She screamed, and they pulled away from each other.

"What are you doing in here?" she demanded.

"Looking for ghosts. Or whatever."

"So were we." She fluffed her hair. "We just got lost."

"Me too." I smiled at Jeremy. "Then, I heard some *activity* and thought maybe there were some ghosts in here. Sorry for interrupting your . . ."

"You're not interrupting anything," he said. "And whether you believe it or not, we did get lost."

"And I was scared." Vanessa gazed up at him in *faux* admiration. "I'm so glad Jeremy was here to protect me."

Just then, the soft hum of music seemed to filter in from above us.

"What the hell is that?" Vanessa asked, and I was almost relieved that she heard it too. "There can't be another room up there."

"There must be." Chills raced along my arms. The sound was still muddled as if broadcast through a time machine.

"All we had to say!" Jeremy shouted. Then, he bolted out of the room.

Vanessa and I stared at each other.

"What did he mean by that?" She tugged at her top, although it didn't appear to need straightening. Believe me, I checked. "I suppose we'd better follow him, don't you think?"

"If we can find the stairs," I said.

"I know where they are."

She led me down a narrow hall and then turned back toward that same dim, watery light I had stepped into when I first arrived on this floor. There was the staircase. I looked up and, yes, there were two or more steps above us, hidden by darkness as thick as fog.

The *Ghost Seekers* crew and most of our classmates hurried to where we stood and swarmed over those steps like ants. I followed them. There must be another room above the one where I'd caught Vanessa making out with Jeremy. And there must have been something in that room. Something that had sent Jeremy running in search of it.

Instead there was only a tiny balcony with windows overlooking the bay. Jeremy stood, his back to me, looking out and pressing his fingers against the dusty glass.

Then, slowly, he turned back, looked around the room, at each of us, and finally, at me.

"Nothing."

"But, Jeremy . . ." Vanessa whined.

He didn't seem to notice. His gaze remained fixed on me.

"Nothing," he repeated, and walked out of the room.

Beside me, Tati slumped to the floor with a moan.

NOTES TO SELF

Tati is fine. She said she's always had fainting spells when she is nervous or upset. It runs in her family, she told me. We are sitting together again, riding back to the college. When we took our seats, she smiled at me and said, "Good material for you," and I could only nod. The heat in the trolley is as close and warm as a sweater, but I'm just now beginning to thaw out. Did we really hear what we thought we did? And why did Jeremy shout, "All we had to say!" and run out of the room? Fixed Air that I am, I can't stop mulling this one.

"Nothing," he had said when he turned from the window, his expression so devastated that I can see it even now. A sane person would stop chewing on it, as my gram would say. A sane person would go back to her room, where her roommate is probably serving Virgo-perfect espresso to Vanessa and Dirk, and maybe even the television crew. A sane person wouldn't worry about Jeremy and where he might be right now. So, why can't I stop thinking about him? Why can't I erase the memory of that look on his face?

9

By now you are no doubt starting to realize that each Sun sign is complex, as individual as each person is. To review, there are four elements: Fire, Earth, Air, and Water. The three qualities are Cardinal, Fixed, and Mutable. Now, let's take a look at the two dualities, Masculine and Feminine. Masculine signs, which are considered more assertive, consist of Aries, Gemini, Leo, Libra, Sagittarius, and Aquarius. That's right—the Fire and Air signs. Thus, the Feminine, more receptive signs are Taurus, Cancer, Virgo, Scorpio, Capricorn, and Pisces, the Earth and Water signs. Planets in Masculine signs are believed to add spirituality as well as physical

AND MENTAL ACTIVITY. THOSE IN FEMININE SIGNS ADD EMPATHY AND INTUITION. WHY DO YOU NEED TO KNOW THIS? BECAUSE EACH SUN SIGN IS MADE UP OF ONE ELEMENT, ONE QUALITY AND ONE DUALITY. AND THAT'S JUST THE SUN! YOU CAN LEARN A GREAT DEAL FROM IT.

—*Fearless Astrology*

o, if I had guessed right about Jeremy, he was a Feminine/receptive Fixed Earth Sign. Maybe there was some balance hiding behind that stubborn attitude after all. I had gone looking for him after he had left the restaurant, but neither he nor Dirk answered when I knocked on the door of their room. I'm not sure what I planned on saying to him. I just wanted to know what he had seen or heard that had upset him so much.

I ended up going back to my room and reading more about dualities. Candice was still out, so I didn't have to hide what I was doing. Not that I was ashamed of it. Other than my two best friends at home, I wasn't comfortable with anybody watching me when I did the astro stuff. That's what I got for being a Masculine, Fixed Air sign, I guess.

In the morning, we all gathered in the cafeteria, the same

as always, but only on the surface. I could tell that something had changed since last night. It was as if the long table had begun to divide like an amoeba. I remained in my same seat on either side of Candice and Tati. Dirk and Vanessa were huddled at the other end, talking quietly. The twins from New York sat to their left but pretended not to notice them. Critter and his roommate Brad, who shaved his head and went by Brad Dog, had not shown up yet. Neither had Mariah, the shy girl with the long bangs. Jeremy sat alone on the patio reading a book. As much as I wanted to approach him, I didn't know how.

"You're looking at him again," Candice said.

"Busted." I turned back to her and Tati. "It's just that he's . . ."

". . . hot," she said.

"I mean, the way he was last night. It was as if . . . "

". . . as if he was on drugs or something."

Just then, I realized that this was a nasty little flaw in Candice's otherwise flawless personality. Although she was trying to be helpful, the way she finished my sentences for me always left them different from what I had intended.

"That's not what I meant," I said. "I don't think Jeremy is on drugs. What I do think is that he saw or heard something in that room that we didn't."

Candice shrugged. "Then, why don't you just ask him?"

Why didn't I? As I considered it, Jeremy got up from the patio table and walked away.

"Hurry," Candice said.

But I couldn't. No, I had to.

Before I could stop myself, I was on my feet and running out onto the patio.

"Jeremy, wait."

He stopped. Turned. "Hey, Logan."

There we were—in front of most of the people from class, all of whom were no doubt watching this drama on the wide screens of the cafeteria windows right now.

"I need to talk to you," I said.

"About?" That Earth sign arrogance again.

"Well, you ran out of the room last night. You said some stuff that didn't make much sense. I was wondering . . ."

". . . There's nothing I can tell you," he said.

"You can if you want to. Come on, Jeremy. What really happened up there?"

"Nothing," he said. "Leave me alone."

Then, in plain view of the world, our world, at least, he turned his back on me and headed toward the classroom.

My face went hot. What a fool I must look like. Someone giggled. I looked back toward the cafeteria, and there was Vanessa, smirk firmly in place, black hair framing her face, matching sweater pulled tight across her chest.

My gram always said, "They can kill you, but they can't eat you." I made myself think about that. Yes, I looked like a fool for coming out there after a guy who clearly wanted nothing to do with me. But my purpose was to find out what had caused him to act the way he had last night. Just maybe I'd have a reason to do that inside under the watchful eye of Jaffa, who if I was right, already kind of liked me.

As we entered the room, I realized that the class had spread out much the same inside as we had in the cafeteria. The New York twins shared a small table with Brad Dog, Critter, and Mariah. Although Tati, Candice, and I still sat together, Vanessa and Dirk had moved dangerously close to us, as if we should all be buddies after what we'd experienced together. Odd that they had distanced themselves from Jeremy, who was now alone at the end of our table, but maybe not after the weird way he had acted last night.

Jaffa walked up to the podium, all business.

"I know we're all excited about what happened at the restaurant last night," he said, "but we have a lot of material we need to cover today."

"Do you think *Ghost Seekers* will film here?" Vanessa asked.

He nodded. "It looks that way. Rik McNeil and the crew are supposed be here next week. Emily told me they want all of us who saw what took place to show up for possible interviews."

"Cool." Vanessa applauded.

She was the only one.

"For now, though," Jaffa said. "We need to move forward. I've got a lot to teach you people and not much time to do it. Today we are going to put the events of last night aside and focus on the basics of interviewing."

"Why?" Vanessa asked. "So that we'll be ready when the TV people come to talk to us?"

"No," Tati shot back. "It's because we're writers, and we should be the ones doing the interviewing."

"Thank you, Tatiyana. Learning how to interview is extremely important, and it's all about getting great quotes and great anecdotes." Jaffa directed a pained glance at Vanessa as if to ask if she was getting it.

She sighed and crossed her arms. "What's an anecdote, exactly?"

Tati groaned. Candice nudged her as if to say *Shut up*.

"Would anyone like to answer Vanessa's question?" Jaffa asked.

"What an idiot," I whispered to Tati. "She doesn't even..."

"Logan, could you please speak up?"

Oh no.

"An anecdote is kind of like a story the person you are interviewing tells you," I said and remembered what Ms. Snider, my journalism teacher at home, had taught me.

"Exactly." He rubbed his hands together. "You go into an interview armed with every imaginable fact. Your job as the interviewer is to learn what you didn't know before that time, what isn't on record. You must get the subject to talk and remember, and yes, Logan, to tell stories. We are going to practice the technique tomorrow."

"What about today?" Vanessa was still obviously pissed that I was getting too much of Jaffa's attention. "I was the one who first sensed Sean Baylor's spirit in that restaurant, after all."

"And Tatiyana will interview you about that tomorrow in class," he said.

Tati made a face. "Why me?"

"Because you sensed Baylor too, didn't you?"

"I sensed something, and maybe heard something, not exactly music. And I am not saying it was Baylor."

"You did faint."

"Sometimes when I'm excited, I forget to breathe. I've been doing it my whole life."

Vanessa whispered something to Dirk.

"Did you have a question?" The tone of Jaffa's voice could have frozen the room.

"No. Sorry, Henry." She looked down at the desk.

"Good. Then, Tatiyana, you will interview Vanessa tomorrow." He turned toward me. "Logan?"

"Yes?"

"You will interview Jeremy."

"No way." Jeremy stared straight at me with such hostility that I had to turn away. "I'm not being interviewed by anybody, especially not . . ."

"Come on," Jaffa interrupted. "I changed some rules for you. Change some for me."

"No, that's not going to work." Jeremy got up from his chair. "I told you I don't want to do it."

"This is my workshop," Jaffa said. "Unfortunately, there is room for only one *prima donna*."

Jeremy didn't seem to hear. He was already on his way out of the room.

"He will be back," Jaffa said. "And, Logan, you will interview him."

"But . . ."

"I said you *will* interview him. He is still a little disturbed about what happened last night, especially since he was so convinced that Sean Baylor's spirit is not in Monterey."

"I don't understand," I said. "Why did he run from the restaurant? And why is he so upset?"

"Because there's a good chance that Baylor's spirit really is here."

"Do you believe that?"

"Emily and Doug do." He shrugged. "And, yes, it's possible. That music we heard was one of his songs. 'All We Had to Say.'"

"That was Baylor's music?" I broke out in chills.

Someone gasped.

"Wow," Vanessa said.

"Enough." Jaffa put up his hands. "It's an exciting possibility, and one that you will have the opportunity of writing about, Logan. But right now, I have a class to conduct. Any objections?"

I shook my head. But all I could think about was that music we'd heard last night. Sean Baylor's music.

NOTES TO SELF

So that's what Jeremy had meant! It was the name of a Baylor song. No wonder he was so upset. He made a big deal of putting down the possibility of Baylor's spirit being here. Now, he's heard Baylor's music with his own ears.

Although Jaffa seems to like him, he wasn't pleased today. If he actually did flush a student's cell phone down a toilet (which I still cannot imagine an Aquarius doing), how will he react to a student walking out at the beginning of class? It doesn't make any sense to me. Jeremy was rude. He made it clear—in front of everyone—that he doesn't want me to interview him. There's only one answer. He has something to hide, and, for some crazy reason, he's afraid that I might discover it.

AS YOU JOURNEY THROUGH LIFE, DON'T BE AFRAID TO TAKE CHANCES. GO WHERE YOU MUST. SAY WHAT YOU MUST. DO WHAT YOU MUST. THIS IS EASIER FOR SOME SIGNS THAN FOR OTHERS. DON'T WORRY ABOUT THAT. BREAK OUT OF ANY SHACKLES—AND EVERY SIGN HAS ITS SPECIAL BRAND OF SHACKLES, WHICH IS A FANCY WORD FOR THE FEARS THAT HOLD US BACK. THE FIRE SIGNS FEAR BEING STOPPED. THE AIR SIGNS FEAR BEING TUNED OUT. THE EARTH SIGNS FEAR BEING WRONG, AND THE WATER SIGNS FEAR BEING DESERTED. DON'T LET YOUR SIGN HOLD YOU BACK. TAKE CHANCES.

—Fearless Astrology

*T*ati, Candice, and I ate lunch together. Later, we returned to the library. They researched. I wrote. And wrote. Before I realized it, most of the day was gone.

"Got to run," Candice said. "Come on, girls. We're having a pizza party in the room tonight."

"We are?" Tati asked.

"We *are*?" I echoed.

"Sorry." She gave me that calm smile, and I wondered how it would be to feel that comfortable in my own skin. "With everything that happened last night, I might have forgotten to mention it. It was so bizarre with the ghost and all. And then the way Jeremy just walked out of class. I wonder if Jaffa will flush him down the toilet."

"That's not funny," I told her.

"You're right." She reached across the table and squeezed my arm. "Sorry, Logan. I know that there's nothing funny when it comes to you and Jeremy."

As if we were a unit.

"I don't know how to answer that," I said.

"You don't have to. You and Tati just try to be back in our room in about . . ." She looked at her watch. ". . . thirty minutes or so. We'll have a great time. The *Ghost Seekers* people will be there. Emily promised they'd drop by."

Once Candice had left, Tati and I walked outside together. The breeze was cold but not uncomfortable, the kind of weather meant for hot chocolate and long baths.

Tati zipped her jacket. "Do you want to go to the pizza thing?"

"I don't know. Vanessa will probably make it a point to show up."

She nodded. "To tell you the truth, let's just say that as a roommate, she sucks."

"I can imagine," I said. *Could I ever.*

"So would you like to ditch the party and work on our articles instead? I don't have a three-thousand dollar espresso machine, but my herb tea is pretty good, if I do say so."

"Work, work, and more work. You've got to be an Earth sign, Tati."

"Capricorn. Don't hate me for it."

And judging by that purple streak, a little fire in there, an Aries or Leo Moon, maybe.

"My journalism teacher back home is a Capricorn," I said. "From what I've read, all of those long hours and fear of poverty get easier to deal with as you get older."

She grinned. "I certainly hope so. Are you sure you don't want to ditch the pizza thing and hang out with me?"

"I need to do something else tonight."

"Looking for Jeremy, aren't you?"

"Am I really that pathetically obvious?"

"Probably not to most folks," she said. "I just can't help watching people. The guy is really into you."

"If you believe that, you must be joining Critter in whatever little activity he engages in before class."

"Critter is the last fool on Earth I'd join for any activity. Jeremy, though. The guy likes you. You like him, too, don't you?"

"I don't know. It's hard to like someone you're in competition with."

"I hear you," she said. "Stop by later if you want. I'll be up late. And I could use some hints about how to win over Jaffa."

"As if I know."

"You do know, Logan. Why do you think the others are so jealous of you?"

Jealous? "What others?" I asked.

"Vanessa, Jeremy, everyone who's hoping to get in that anthology."

"Are you sure about that?"

She nodded. "Believe it, girl. Anyone else who came in late the way you did yesterday would have gotten kicked out on the spot."

She had a point there. "Thanks for telling me that. You are the first person here who has actually given me any hope."

"I've got your back," she said. "This workshop is far from over, and some of these people would like to see you fail big time. Instead of looking for Jeremy, maybe you should just try to get some rest."

"Sure," I said and heard her laughter as I walked away.

I found him on the beach that night—the same place as the first time we had met out there past the ice plant and the sand dunes. He had built a little fire in a pit and was sitting on a rock facing it. I stopped, aware that I was invading his privacy. No. I needed to do this. He had a secret he felt I was too close to figuring out, and I had to convince him to share it.

As I got closer, I realized that he was holding something that appeared to be real food. What did this Earth sign have that smelled so wonderful?

He turned almost as if he expected me to be standing there, and got up. "Have some fish and chips." He walked over to me and held out the container. "My favorite."

Mine too. So that's what the irresistible scent was. Taurus comfort food, for sure. I imagined how it would taste to bite into a vinegary potato wedge and then forced myself to delete the image.

"I don't think so," I said. "You were terrible to me in class today."

"I had a pretty terrible night. You can be pushy when you want something."

Pushy? Me?

"I didn't know what was going on," I said, trying to defend myself from his unflattering assessment. "Do you think it's true that Baylor's spirit is in that restaurant?"

"I've never believed it. Come on, have some fish. There are two left." He lifted out a crispy piece and handed it to me.

I took it in spite of myself. I couldn't help it. "Thanks."

I crunched into the fish, followed Jeremy closer to the fire, and sat down on a large rock in front of him. Then I noticed a guitar leaning against it. "You came out here to play?"

"Tonight I did." The guarded look returned. "So, what are *you* doing here?"

"I wanted to let you know that Jaffa told us about that being a Baylor song we heard last night."

"'All We Had to Say.' That's why I . . ." He stopped.

"It all makes sense now. At the time, I didn't know what was going on. You must have been the only one who recognized it."

"Of course I was. But I didn't go running up there to find the ghost of Sean Baylor."

"Why, then?"

"I thought I might be able to . . ." He stopped abruptly.

". . . What? Why did you go up there, and why did you look so miserable when you turned around from the window?"

"It's complicated," he said.

"Try to tell me. My dad says the only thoughts and experiences that own you are the ones of which you cannot speak."

It was difficult to read his expression. Finally, he said, "Sounds as if you have a pretty cool dad."

"I do." For some reason, my throat caught when I said it.

"By the way, why didn't you didn't tell me that you were going to the newspaper office yesterday morning?"

"We haven't been exactly working together," I said. "Why didn't you tell *me* you went there the day before?"

"I probably should have. You know, we don't really need to compete, Logan. All you care about is the astrology stuff, and I'm only interested in what really happened."

"You don't think astrology is real?"

"Do you?"

"You think I'm faking it?" I asked. "I'll admit I don't know how it works, and I only recently started studying it."

"Then how do you explain that other people with the same birthday as mine are totally different?"

"Lots of reasons. They could have a different Moon, a different Rising sign."

"That's just a crock, and you know it."

"No it is not." I stood up, and he did the same. "I'll bet every one of those people you're thinking about isn't *entirely* different from you. I'll bet you share similar traits."

"You're pretty good." He grinned. "If I didn't know better, you'd have me convinced that you really do believe that stuff."

"Why would I pretend?"

"To have a gimmick to set you off from everyone else and give yourself a better chance to be published in the anthology."

I felt my face grow hot, the way it had when he humiliated me outside the cafeteria. "A gimmick like Sean Baylor?"

"He's not."

"Neither is astrology. And I don't appreciate being called a fake."

"You used the word. I didn't."

"But it's what you meant." I no longer cared what he thought. I might as well go for it. "If I'm such a fake, explain to me how I've known you less than a week and can already tell that you're a Taurus."

He looked as if I'd caught him without any clothes on.

"What are you talking about?"

"Your Sun sign," I said. "You were born between April 20 and May 20, weren't you?"

"There's no way you could possibly . . ."

I was right. *Thank you, gram Janie.* "From what I know about you, it's entirely possible that you could be a double Taurus with . . ." I squinted at him and tried to channel my gram. ". . . Maybe some Fire, an Aries Moon, maybe. Leo, even."

"So, what'd you do?" he asked with that same smirky smile. "Look up my birthday in the class records?"

"Do you really think I'd go to all of that trouble, even if I knew how to do it?"

"I'm not sure." For the first time since we were thrown together in the seat on that bus, he looked uncertain. "Right now, all I know is that you have information about me that you shouldn't have. Information you couldn't have gotten by guesswork."

"Well, give me your birth date, and I'll be able to tell you even more."

"No thanks," he said. "If you want more, you'll need to do whatever you did to find out my sign."

"If that's how you want to behave," I told him. "And by the way, Sean Baylor was a Gemini. Any time you'd like to hear more about him, I'd be happy to discuss it with you."

"I'm not interested in any of that."

"Let me know if you change your mind. I'm really cool

about sharing anything, because I am not threatened by you."

"And I'm not threatened by you."

"That's not the way it appears," I said. "But thanks for keeping your promise about the book. I had better get back now. See you in class."

"Maybe," he said. "Maybe not. Just so you know, not everybody is all that pleased about Jaffa believing that astro stuff of yours."

A nice parting shot. Being a Taurus, Jeremy had probably planned it in advance. Being an Aquarius, I decided to mull it over before blurting out a barrage of questions.

"I don't care what they think about me. I'm here to work with Jaffa."

"Yeah, right."

I'd had enough of his attitude. "Believe what you like. I'm leaving now."

"You don't have to walk back alone," he said. "I borrowed Dirk's car."

"It's not far to the dorms, and I'll be okay. All of the ghosts seem to be hanging out at the restaurant these days." I meant it as a kind of joke to ease the tension between us, but the moment I spoke, I realized that it made me sound like a smart ass.

"Fine," he said. "I'm not going to argue with you."

"Okay, then." I started off across the beach.

Jeremy didn't try to stop me again. Why should he? He had made his point. How could he possibly believe that I was faking astrology? He was the one who was faking it—pretending to like me, offering me food, the Taurus equivalent of gold. And all of the time, he had believed that I was a fake.

The walk back was creepier than getting to the beach had been. The fog began to roll in. As I made my way through the dunes, I realized that it was getting really dark out here. And cold. And a little scary. I should have brought my flashlight.

Then, I felt it again—that icy, uneasy presence. *Just ignore it*, I told myself. *Just keep walking. Only five minutes to the dorm.*

A freezing ocean breeze cut through me. I dug my hands deeper in my jacket. The wind played games with my head. It sounded kind of like music. Muted music from someone's dorm room, except there was no dorm, no room, no anything. Only the trees, the ice plant, and the darkness.

The voice was thin and far away. Chills sprouted along my arms, and I tried to make out the words.

> *Was all we had to say to each other*
> *all we had to say to each other?*
> *Was forever only a feeling we shared for just one night?*

As suddenly as it began, it stopped. I tried to rub away the chills and couldn't. I'd heard the music, the guitar, a man's soft voice. No way could I hold back any longer. I screamed. I tried to run, to get away from the music, back the way I had come. I struggled through the sand and ran into a wall. A human wall.

"You're okay. I'm here." Jeremy held me tightly against him.

I managed to lift my head. "Did you hear that? The song?"

"Yeah. I followed you." He pressed me harder to his chest. "I wanted to be sure you got back to the dorm."

"Thank you." I clung to him and relished the warmth. "I was so scared. I can't tell you how scared I was."

"Don't be." He lifted my chin and forced me to look into his eyes. "Whatever it is, Logan, it's not real. It can't be."

"I'm not so sure," I said. Yet I continued to cling to him.

NOTES TO SELF

I can still feel Jeremy's arms around me—still smell the ocean and that wonderful scent he was wearing. There was not a trace of that smug Taurus who had broken Jaffa's rules. Only after he made sure that I was all right, had he let go of me and gone after whoever had been playing the music. He was convinced somebody was trying to scare us. I wasn't so sure and stood shivering until he returned and admitted that he hadn't been able to find anybody out there.

We didn't say anything on the way back to the car, but he kept his arm firmly around me until we got there. I did not object. And, yes, I probably should have. I couldn't, though. I was scared, and walking that close to him made me feel momentarily safe. Lucky for me that I'll be going home this weekend. Away from here, them, and him. I am so ready to get back to real life.

PICTURE YOUR MOON AS A COLOR BLENDED INTO YOUR
SUN SIGN. IS IT BRIGHT AND FULL OF FIRE? GLITTERY
AND INSUBSTANTIAL AS AIR? SOLID AS EARTH WITH
LITTLE VARIANCE? DEEP AS WATER? THAT COLOR
COMPLEMENTS, STRENGTHENS, OR MODIFIES YOUR
SUN SIGN. EMBRACE YOUR MOON. IT ADDS NUANCES
AND EMOTION TO THE ELEMENTS, QUALITIES, AND
DUALITIES OF YOUR SUN.

—Fearless Astrology

     ince my gram first wrote *Fearless*, it had gotten
much easier to figure out Moon signs, not to mention
Mars, Venus, and the rest. All I had to do was a search
for "free astrology charts," on the Internet. Sure, they all
wanted to sell something, but I didn't have to buy.

I had figured out my Moon sign when I had first discovered the book. Emotional, watery Pisces, but that wasn't all that bad for a Fixed Air Aquarius Sun. I wondered what Jeremy's Moon was and guessed Fire. He was more aggressive than a lot of the Earth signs I'd known. I hoped he would be more Earth and less Fire today in class. Interviewing him could make me forget how good it felt when he had held me last night.

Vanessa was actually wearing a turtleneck, but, in all fairness to her usual me-me-me, it was a red turtleneck that only intensified her long, black hair. And it did have a zipper up the front.

In my regulation Writers Camp T-shirt and teal jacket, I felt pretty bland by comparison. I had to smile, though. Jaffa was wearing Air sign colors, too. But that navy scarf of his was pure, emotional Water. I needed to figure out his Moon.

Vanessa chattered with Candice about a play they were going to see downtown. I wondered when she had time to write. She continued talking until Jaffa cleared his throat.

"We will have two interviews today." He gave the scarf a fond pat. "You will all take notes, and so will each of the interviewers. The more skilled you are as writers, the more your diverse your finished articles will be. Pay special attention to getting down direct quotes and any anecdotes the speaker reveals."

"You mean stories about various situations?" Vanessa asked, and I knew she was trying to mimic what I had said earlier.

"Whatever you can get out of the subject," he said.

"Remember, facts are easy to find, and anyone can locate and write them down. A good reporter gets the quote no one else could have gotten. That story that the subject has never before revealed to anyone."

I tried to write as fast as he talked. These tips might make me look older than an incoming high school junior when I interviewed Mercedes next week.

"Logan and Tatiyana, I'm impressed," he said. "You two are the only ones taking notes right now."

"I have my recorder on." Vanessa announced with pride. "Isn't that the same thing?"

"It's good for backup, of course. But it's a secondary skill to taking good notes."

Vanessa flounced around in her chair and pulled a multi-colored notebook out of her bag. "So, when's the assignment due?"

"Monday. Does that work for you?"

Big pout. Imagining her social calendar. "I guess so."

"Then why don't we start the first interview with Logan and Jeremy."

"Henry, wait." Vanessa raised her hand, but didn't pause for him to acknowledge her. "Before we go on with these interviews, don't you think we need to talk about what happened last night?"

"And that was?" His voice took on a tone of mild irritation.

"Didn't you hear? Baylor's spirit was back in the restaurant again."

"It was?" Jaffa glared around the room. "Did any of you

know this? It's extremely important to speak up about any occurrence."

"I think I heard him," Candice finally said. "We went there for dessert right after our pizza party."

"Thank you, Candice." Jaffa shot her a smile. "You must all come forward with anything you experience, even if you're not sure what it means. Anyone else?"

I glanced at Jeremy. He looked down, his message to me was clear.

I was probably out of my mind for doing this, but Jaffa was serious about wanting information, and I had to tell the truth. If it came out later, he would be furious.

"Logan?"

Jaffa must have read the look on my face. I nodded and said, "I heard something too."

Jeremy shot me a warning look. I ignored it.

"You did?" Jaffa asked. "What happened? Where were you?"

"Walking back across the beach last night. I heard music. It was that song, 'All We Had to Say.' I heard a man's voice singing it, and then it was gone."

"And you were alone?"

"Not exactly. I mean, I thought I was alone. I didn't realize that Jeremy had followed me, but he heard it too. We both did."

Vanessa gasped.

"Is that right, Jeremy?" he asked. "Did you hear the music as well?"

"I heard something." Jeremy glared at me. "A radio, maybe. Not a ghost. Just normal music."

"Sean Baylor's music?"

"I'm not sure."

"Of course, you're sure," I said. "We discussed it. You went crazy trying to find out where it was coming from."

"You're really exaggerating this, Logan. It was someone with a radio."

"When was the last time a Baylor song was played on any radio station?" I turned to Jaffa, who was the one taking rapid notes now. "We couldn't find where it was coming from, and while it may not have been a Baylor's ghost, it was weird."

"So you two were out there together?" Vanessa's cheeks were now almost as red as her sweater.

"Yes." I smiled at her. I couldn't help it. "I heard the music after I started back toward the dorms."

"So, you were on a date?" Her expression was pretty scary. "That's why you weren't at the pizza party?"

I remembered that it wasn't a good idea to tangle with an Aries, especially over a love object, which Jeremy apparently was, to her, at least.

"We ran into each other out there, that's all. I headed back to the dorms, and before I got there, the music started. Jeremy heard me scream, and we walked back to Dirk's car together."

She shot Dirk a look and then focused on Jaffa again. "So how is that possible, Henry? If Logan is telling the truth, she and Jeremy heard Sean Baylor's song about the same time that all of us at the restaurant did."

"I'm not sure how that works," he said. "It's my understanding that spirits are trapped souls. Thus, it doesn't seem that they could appear in more than one location at the same time."

"All I know is that it was that song we heard at the restaurant." I looked over at Jeremy then back at him.

"Where did you go after that?" Vanessa asked, which made me both blush and want to smack her.

Jaffa seemed to sense it. "Actually, Logan should be asking the questions," he said. "After the break, Tatiyana will interview you, Vanessa. Then you will all write your versions of the interview. Are you ready, Logan?"

"Yes."

"Jeremy?"

He shrugged and walked to the front of the room. I did the same. He hadn't even taken off his jacket, as if ready to bolt at any moment. The look he shot me was far from friendly.

I ignored it and focused on the first rule of interviewing; bond with the subject. *Right.*

"Hi, Jeremy. Now, that I've been studying Sean Baylor, I can see why you're so involved in him."

"Why's that?"

Who elected him interviewer? "Well, as a musician yourself, you no doubt have an appreciation of his musical abilities. When did you first become interested in him?"

"I always have been."

"You've made it clear that you don't think Sean Baylor's spirit is in Monterey. Why is that?"

"Because it isn't."

"What do you think you and I heard last night?"

"A radio," he said. "With all the ghost talk, maybe the stations dug up some of his music. Or maybe you did."

I heard a titter that could only have come from Vanessa. That did it. Forget his arm around me. Forget how close I felt to him. He was making me look bad in front of Jaffa.

"Last night, after I screamed and you caught up with me, you said it wasn't real. What did you mean by that?"

"You know what I meant." He shoved his hands into the pocket of his jacket. "That it wasn't a ghost."

"Are you saying a ghost is real?"

"No." His eyes were blazing, but his voice was cool and in control. "I meant that someone was playing Baylor's music. That's why I ran off to see where it was coming from."

"What did you find?"

"Nothing," he said. "Which makes me wonder. I mean, you were the only person around. And all of a sudden, there's his song, right where you happen to be walking."

I could not believe what he was implying. He couldn't possibly. I needed every ounce of my Aquarian cool.

"And how do you explain the music at the restaurant?" I asked.

"I don't know." He glanced at Tati and held her gaze for a moment. "If someone wanted to stage Baylor sightings, I guess they would need an accomplice to fake-haunt the other place. I would start by looking at whoever *wasn't* at the pizza party."

"For what possible reason?" I could barely keep it together now. I glanced up and saw, to my horror, that even Critter was staring at me with open curiosity. No time to ponder. "Why would anyone, with or without an accomplice, want to fake something like that?"

"You got me there." Those eyes I'd once thought sexy grew even more pale and clearly hostile. "But then I'm not the one who brought up the topic."

NOTES TO SELF

Jeremy hates me. Whatever I thought was happening out there on the beach between us was killed when I told Jaffa the truth about hearing Baylor's music. Jeremy forced me to be tough; I didn't have any choice. Now, he's suggesting that I—and maybe Tati and I—faked the music. What a rotten interviewer I am. Jaffa is going to think I'm the biggest loser on the planet. How am I going to be able to walk back in that room after the break?

12

EVERY CAPRICORN WANTS TO BE THE BEST AT SOME-
THING, EVEN SOMETHING AS MINOR AS MOWING THE
GRASS. EVERY SIGN WANTS TO SUCCEED. THERE'S A
DIFFERENCE, THOUGH. THE EARTH SIGNS, ESPECIALLY
CAPRICORN, ARE MORE PRACTICAL. UNEVOLVED
EARTH SIGNS, HOWEVER, THINK BY STAYING BUSY,
PUTTING IN LONG HOURS, AND MAKING DETAILED
LISTS ARE THE WAY TO GET THERE. UNEVOLVED FIRE
SIGNS TRY TO TAKE SHORTCUTS, OR THEY WORK FOR
THE LIMELIGHT ALONE. AND, OF COURSE, THE AIR
SIGNS WILL TALK ABOUT SUCCESS, AS IF IT IS THEIR
NEW BEST FRIEND, AS THE WATER SIGNS HOPE FOR IT
AND THEN SAY IT REALLY DOESN'T MATTER.

—Fearless Astrology

on't let Jeremy get to you." I realized that Tati had followed me out on the patio. "He was a real ass in there. Can you imagine what everyone else must be thinking about us?"

"It makes me sick. You know they're all talking about it." How could I go back in that room and face the kids who were going to write their versions of that so-called interview?

"The good news is that I get to interview Vanessa after the break." The Capricorn grinned as if waiting for me to say something.

"Meaning?"

"Meaning that you must have some trash on that chick."

"Nothing that you don't already have."

"Come on. She's probably the reason your guy turned against you. Tell me whatever you know, and I'll use it when I interview her."

"You are going to be a great investigative reporter, Tati."

Clearly, that wasn't what she had expected me to say. "How's that?"

"Jaffa told us in the first class meeting. The best way for an investigative reporter to get information is to find an angry person."

"That wasn't what I was trying to do." The wind kicked up. The purple streak in her hair didn't move. "Did it work?"

"Maybe. Just ask her what they were doing upstairs in the restaurant when they heard Sean Baylor's music."

"Oh, really?" She giggled. "That girl is terrible."

"With you doing the interviewing, everyone just might find out how terrible," I said. "Then, maybe we won't look so guilty by comparison."

Once we were back in the classroom, we all spread around the room watching Vanessa, who had already bounced up to the podium. She'd pulled that dark hair up into a ponytail, which made her look both innocent and sexy. Did the self-involved Aries think Jaffa was going to film this interview?

Tati joined them in front, and I sat down in back.

"Are you ready?" Jaffa asked from the head of the table.

"Ready," Vanessa said.

"Tatiyana, you are the interviewer." He nodded at her. "Let's begin."

She joined Vanessa, and the rest of us got ready to take notes. "All right," she said. "Thanks for speaking with me today, Vanessa."

Another rule: Be gracious to the source. And Capricorn follows the rules.

"Yeah, right."

And yet another: Aries doesn't always follow the rules.

Tati glanced at Jaffa, who nodded.

"It's fine," he said. "You may indeed encounter hostile sources. That's part of being a strong interviewer, getting the source to open up."

"Well, then," Tati said, but I could see that she was shaken by Vanessa's nastiness. "What do you remember about the night that we heard Sean Baylor's music? You seemed pretty certain that he was in the restaurant."

"How can you even ask questions about that night?" she snapped. "You were passed out like a drunk in an alley."

Tati gasped and went speechless.

"Well *I* wasn't passed out," I said, "and Tati is right. You were extremely vocal about Baylor's spirit being there."

"Isn't this cheating, Henry?" Vanessa's confidence seemed to fading right along with her lip gloss. "Logan's trying to bail her out."

"Not at all," he said. "As writers, you'll all encounter many situations where you may need to work with another reporter. Logan, why don't you join Tatiyana?"

"No," Vanessa and I replied almost in unison.

All I had done was try to help out Tati, and now I was going to have to face the class where Jeremy had humiliated me twenty minutes earlier. I walked to the front of the room like an unwilling robot.

Tati flashed me a look of camaraderie. The little outburst I had created had given her time to regroup.

"My first question is about Baylor's ghost," she said. "When did you first sense it, Vanessa?"

"Last weekend, our first night here. On the bus." She sneaked a look at Jaffa. "That's when I first knew that Sean Baylor's spirit was trapped in that restaurant, and that . . ."

"I think Tatiyana is asking when you were first aware of it on Wednesday," I said.

"Right." Tati glanced down at her notebook. It probably looked professional to everyone else, but I knew that she was trying to keep from laughing.

"I was aware the minute we walked in the door," Vanessa said.

"Was that when you first heard the music?" I asked her.

"Of course not. The music didn't start until later."

"Where were you then?"

"You know where."

"She might, but I don't." Tati gave her a strictly business Capricorn smile.

"I was upstairs with Jeremy and Logan."

"Is that so?" Tati glanced back down at her notebook as if trying to figure it out. "Weren't you and Jeremy in the room alone before the music started?"

"Not that I recall." Her eyes darted to Jaffa.

"Logan?" Tati asked.

"As I recall . . ." I couldn't help mimicking Vanessa. ". . . Vanessa and Jeremy were alone in the room. I turned on the light, and not long after that, we heard the music."

The class murmured. I had made my point.

Tati flashed me a victorious grin. "What makes you think the ghost was Sean Baylor's?"

Vanessa's cheeks blazed. "I already told you. It was the music and the fact that I sensed his spirit earlier." She stood. "I've had about enough of this. Why is it all of a sudden such a big deal that I got lost and ended up alone?"

"Alone with Jeremy," Tati said.

I could feel his glare burning into my back, and I didn't dare turn around.

Jaffa didn't look all that happy. Perhaps he categorized students making out during class trips the same way he did cell phones and tardiness.

"Class," he said, "this is still part of the interview, so please continue to take notes and quotes, the way you would with any other source."

"I said I've had enough, Henry."

"This is my class." Although he spoke in a soft, friendly voice, I could see that both of them were ready to go head-to-head.

"In case you don't know, Logan," she said. "The reason I got lost is because I saw something in the hall. It looked like a man."

"Wow," Critter said. The sound of whispering grew loud enough to get a threatening stare from Jaffa. Then the room fell silent again.

"Why didn't you say so at the time?" I asked.

"I forgot."

"You forgot," I repeated, in case anyone had missed it. "What did this ghost man look like?"

"Like Sean Baylor."

"Oh, really? In what way?"

"The guitar. Yes, it kind of looked like he was carrying a guitar."

"Could you see his features?"

"No. It was too dark." She shot me a defiant look. "But I know it was Baylor. If you hadn't been passed out, Tatiyana, you might have seen him too."

"Wait just a minute," I said, ready to point out the difference between passing out and making out.

"Time's up," Jaffa said. "Excellent interview. Thank you Tatiyana, Vanessa, and Logan. Class, I hope you've all taken good notes today. Assignments are due on Monday. Enjoy your weekend off."

Candice, Tati, and I took our time leaving. Once we stepped out of the classroom, I realized that Vanessa was waiting at the door.

She had let her dark hair down, and the wind whipped it against her face.

"You made a big mistake today, Logan." Her smile was manic. "And, in case you didn't notice, you made an enemy."

"If you're speaking about yourself, that's nothing new."

"I'm talking about *him*."

"I can speak for myself." There he was, just steps from me.

"Oh, Jeremy," Vanessa began. "I didn't . . .'"

"I want to talk to Logan." He didn't need to add *alone*. His voice made it clear.

"Fine." She shot me a triumphant smile and walked off behind Tati and Candice.

"Did you hear what she said?" I asked him. "About you being my enemy?"

"Did you hear what I said?" His voice was so angry that he

might as well have been shouting. "About being able to speak for myself? That was a cheap shot you took in there, and I know you and Tatiyana had it planned."

"What about you, Jeremy? You tried to make everyone think that I had played that music out there on the beach."

"Maybe you did."

"Think whatever you like." I started to move down the path, toward the dorms. "At least I didn't try to make them believe that you were playing the music." Now there was a thought.

"Wait a minute. I told you why Vanessa and I were in that room at the restaurant. You tried to turn it into something else to discredit me in front of Jaffa."

"All I did was tell what I saw. Your little Aries friend is the one who lied. And if you believe she was really lost and scared, you need to read up on Fire signs."

"I am so sick of you trying to make points with that phony astro stuff."

Now the Bull was raging. Time for this Aquarius to leave.

"If you think I am trying to make points with you, you are very wrong." I kept my voice calm. "I'll be researching Sean Baylor this weekend. See you on Monday."

"You don't even care about Sean Baylor." He grabbed my arm.

"Let go of me."

"Take your hands off of her, you jerk." All of a sudden, there was Chili, my best friend from home—all attitude, wild highlights flashing in her dark hair. She flung herself against us and broke his hold.

"She's all yours." Jeremy stepped back and looked at both of us with disgust.

I no longer cared.

"Chili," I gasped. "You're really here."

"I sure am. Paige and I got away early. I'm so glad we did. What's going on?"

"Everything." Then I saw Paige running down the path. She was wearing one of her wild designs, and her long, pale hair flew behind her.

"Logan." She looked into my eyes, and I remembered that I could never hide anything from her. "What's wrong, Logan? You're not crying?"

"No." I hugged her, hugged Chili, and held my breath waiting for them to start chattering. Within seconds, they did.

"I missed you so much," Chili said. "My mom sent food."

"I missed you, too. Who's the guy?"

"Quiet, Paige," Chili whispered. "Wait until we're out of here."

Finally, we were inside Chili's silver Spyder—me beside Chili, and Paige in the back—just like always. The car hummed to life. Soon, we'd be home, where maybe I could just hang out and think about everything that had happened this week. Maybe I could even find out what my dad remembered about Sean Baylor.

"That guy could have hurt you," Chili said. "He must be on something."

"No, he's not." I realized that I was trying to defend Jeremy, but couldn't help myself. "It's just that we're both trying to write about the same topic, and he's pretty competitive."

"I'd stay away from him." Chili reached over and squeezed my shoulder. "He looks like trouble."

I patted her hand and tried to think of a topic guaranteed to distract a Gemini. "Enough about him," I said. "Now, tell me about you and Trevor."

Then, finally, I dared to glance out the car window. Jeremy was still there, all right, glaring back at me. And even at that safe distance, the darkness in his eyes was frightening.

NOTES TO SELF

I am thrilled to be with my very best friends again. It's get-real time for me, and as much as I love Jaffa's workshop, no one there, not even Candice and Tati, measures up to Paige and Chili. We talked nonstop during the ride home. Chili wanted me to understand that the breakup with Trevor isn't her fault. She just couldn't stand that secretive Scorpio. Paige is still happy with Hunter, her hard-working Aries boyfriend.

And what about me? They asked. Was I still interested in my old boyfriend Nathan? Not after the way he lied to me. Had I met anyone?

Actually, I'm a little more interested in Jeremy than I should be. I can't believe I just admitted that to myself.

13

IN TIMES OF TROUBLE, STAY TRUE TO YOUR SUN SIGN.
IF YOU ARE FIRE—BLAZE. IF YOU ARE EARTH—STAY
STRONG. IF YOU ARE WATER—SWIM. AND IF YOU ARE
AIR—SPEAK YOUR MIND.

—Fearless Astrology

ell, I guess that made it pretty clear. I was an Air sign, and I had started speaking my mind. It was time for more of the same. It was also time for me to get more proactive and figure out what had really happened to Sean Baylor. Somewhere, someone knew the truth about him. It wasn't Jeremy, and it certainly wasn't Vanessa.

The one person who just might remember him was my Virgo father. Last night, he had a fabulous meal set out for my friends and me when got home. Steak, pilaf, and spinach salad with cranberries, pecans, and blue cheese. Sure, Stella and Andy, Chili's mom and dad, had helped him prepare it, but he had made the effort, in spite of his long hours at the ad agency. It felt good to walk into our house and smell the warm, comforting scent of all of my favorite foods.

Although it was early for a weekend, I got up that morning, put on my Writers Camp tee and jeans, and hoped I would find him in the kitchen. He must be about the right age to remember Baylor.

"What do you mean, you can't be home?" The moment I heard his angry voice, I stopped in the hall. "This is our daughter, in case you've forgotten, Tess. She's home for her first weekend from camp, and *you* can't be?"

I held my breath. He and Mom were fighting again.

"But you promised Logan." He lowered his voice, and I strained to hear. "I'm not sure how long I can keep doing this, Tess."

Then silence. One of them must have hung up.

I turned and headed back down the hall toward my room. No way did I want to put pressure on their relationship. Yet I had, because my mom couldn't come home this weekend, and because he knew I had hoped she could.

"Logan, where do you think you're going?"

I composed a happy face then turned. In blue jeans and a T-shirt, he stood in front of the kitchen counter looking a little lost. "I came back to get my baseball cap," I said. "Chili and Paige are coming to pick me up."

"Cool. Want waffles and bacon?"

"Not today, Dad. No time."

I went back for my cap and then joined him in the kitchen. He'd piled toast on a dish, and I doctored it the way he liked it, with strawberry jam and a smear of peanut butter.

He sat on the stool across from the counter, took a bite of toast and smiled at me. "You got my foodie gene. That's for sure."

"Dad," I said, and felt suddenly shy. "I need to ask you something."

He took another bite of toast. "If it's about your mom and me, give it time, honey. That's what we're doing. This is a big adjustment for all of us."

My eyes stung, but I forced myself to sound upbeat. "Actually, I wanted to talk to you about Sean Baylor, a folk singer who died back in the sixties."

"What about him?" He seemed relieved that I had moved to a safer subject.

"Do you remember his music?"

"Sure. At one time, I had a record of his, I think. It's probably still around here."

That's what I had counted on. He may be a pack rat, but he was an organized one.

"Do you think you can find it now?"

"I have to leave," he said, "but I'll look later. Why are you interested in such an obscure singer?"

"He's the subject of my article for Henry Jaffa's class."

That seemed to please him. "So you're writing about

music instead of that astrology stuff. Good for you."

"Don't mean to disappoint you, Dad, but Jaffa assigned the topic. I'd rather stick pins in my eyes."

"Don't talk like that." He got up from the counter and began shoving glasses into the dishwasher. I wondered what was making him so nervous. Did he believe that delivering Sean Baylor to me would make up for the fact that he hadn't been able to deliver my mom?

I wanted to tell him it was all right. I wanted to say that I loved both of them, and that, sure, I'd adore having a full-time mom the way Chili and Paige did. But I was okay with the way things were. More okay than I had been when Mom had been stuck home and miserable because she couldn't pursue her dream of playing professional golf.

"Dad," I said. "I'm intrigued by astrology. Henry Jaffa is interested in it too. If I can prove myself to him, he might be willing to mentor me."

"What's that going to take, honey? Because, whatever it is, I promise you we will make it happen."

"I'm in competition with another writer." *No need to mention he's a hot guy writer.* "He has sources I don't. Whatever you can dig up about Baylor will help a lot."

"I'll find that record this morning. It's one thing I can do for you."

"You do a lot of things for me."

He gave me a strangely sad look.

Just then, Chili's car pulled into our drive.

"I have to go," I said.

He gave me a hug. "Have fun. Remember what I told you."

I couldn't deal with what was really happening here. I couldn't deal with how alone he was, and how very much he was trying to hide it from me.

"I'll be back in time for dinner."

"Great. Stella and Andy invited us over. They miss you."

"Could we go out, just the two of us?" I asked. And because he got that fearful look he'd had when I caught him on the phone, I added, "I'd like to hear what you remember about Baylor."

"We can't cancel so late. How about breakfast tomorrow?"

"Okay, then." I wondered if his smile was as phony as mine; I wondered if there was a conversation we needed to have, and if either of us had enough honest words for it.

I wasn't about to tell my friends how rotten I felt. It was enough to be with them. Paige had swept her pale hair up into a spiky pouf in back and was actually wearing makeup. I was betting the glasses would be the next to go. Chili wore a black sweater and a scarf that picked up the gold-bronze streaks in her hair. As happy as I was to be with them, I couldn't help worrying about my dad. What would happen to him if my mom left for good? What would happen to me?

We headed to Java & Jazz, where Nathan, my former boyfriend, was supposed to hang out every day. He wasn't there. Neither was anyone else we knew.

"It's changed," I told Chili.

"It's the same as it was a week ago," she said. "You're the one who's changed."

"I haven't."

"Sure you have. You like that weird guy, doesn't she, Paige?"

"He's hot," Paige said. "Those eyes."

"But he grabbed Logan."

"Oh," I said. "*That* weird guy. His name is Jeremy, and he grabbed my arm because I was screaming at him."

"Nathan never grabbed you," Chili said. "Which is another reason that we should wait a little longer. I kind of promised him that we'd be here today."

Nathan had done worse than grab me. He had betrayed me.

"I think I'd like to go home." I got up from the table. "I appreciate your concern, but I don't want to hang out waiting for a guy who thinks I'm only here because of him."

"Logan . . ."

"I mean it," I said.

Chili looked at me as if I were the most clueless person on earth. "So you really don't care about meeting up with Nathan?"

"No. I really don't."

"All right, if that's the way you want it."

"Come on," I said. "This isn't easy for me. You dumped Trevor because he was too secretive. Compare that with what Nathan did to me."

"Okay. I respect that you don't want to see him. And, Logan, I shouldn't have said what I did just now. If you like the weird guy in Monterey, that's all right too."

"Jeremy is not weird," I said. "He's just different."

"And, as I said, hot." Paige the Pisces was getting more assertive. She was almost standing up to Chili.

And poor Chili was just feeling bad because she'd broken up with Trevor.

"If you want a guy who opens up more," I told her, "you ought to find a nice Sagittarius. That's your opposite sign."

"How do I find one?"

"Look for someone who laughs and talks a lot. Possibly someone who likes to travel."

"You're on." She shook that vibrant mass of hair, and began to look like the old Chili again. "I feel better already."

Want to cure a Gem of a broken heart? Just mention the possibility of a new love.

"Me, too," I said.

"So do you mind if we stay a little longer?"

"Let's stay, Logan," Paige said. "It reminds me of this spring—all of that crazy stuff we did. And the guys . . ."

"One relationship out of three that is still working out." Chili could always make me laugh, even when I was laughing at myself. Talking to Paige and her reminded me of how it felt to want only a cute guy and a fellowship to a writers camp.

"Sure," I said.

We had just sat back down when the door opened, and Nathan walked in. His Leo mane of blond hair had started to grow back, and he looked different, older and, if possible, even better than before.

He glanced at our table and lit up when he saw me.

I smiled and took a step toward him.

"Logan," he said. "You look wonderful."

"You too, Nathan."

He beamed. "Chili told me that you were going to be here. Sorry I'm late, but I . . ."

"So, there you are." Standing in the doorway, her long legs covered by a tight pair of jeans and most of her streaked blonde hair hidden by a cap, was Geneva Hamilton. She looked just as feline, just as smug, and just as shameless as when she'd taken him away from me at the end of the school year.

Nathan was speechless. Clearly, she'd followed him here. He looked back and forth, from her to me, then back at her again.

"This was where I left off," I said. "Come on, girls."

"I'm sorry," Chili whispered once we were outside. "He told us they had broken up. You are all he could talk about. I know he wanted to see you."

"Only if he could have sneaked out to do it," I told her. "I'm glad that I didn't make a complete fool out of myself twice. Once was bad enough."

When we got back home, my dad was gone. Probably at the advertising agency where he spent most of his life designing labels for wine bottles. One of those bottles was sitting on top of a piece of paper, the way he always left notes for me.

Back in time for dinner at the C's. I thought you might enjoy looking at this.

"What is it?" Chili asked.

I held up the record album. *"Sean Baylor at the 1967 Monterey Pop Festival,"* I read. "Oh, Chili, this is what I need. We've got to find a way to play it."

"Good luck." She picked up the album and stared at the cover. "I've got to say, he was sexy. They both were."

"Both?"

She turned it around so that I could see. The black-and-white design was as artistic as one of my dad's wine labels—all shadow and light with a squiggle of violet here and there. It illuminated the face of a beautiful dark-haired girl who was shaking a tambourine. She and three blondes—all tangled curls and large lined eyes—leaned in toward the duo on stage.

A skinny guy playing a guitar, faced the microphone, dark hair flying. Beside him was a drummer, clearly slamming. His large Afro was lit in hues of purple.

"What's wrong," Chili asked. "You look as if you've seen . . ." She stopped abruptly.

"No," I said. "Not a ghost. Far from it. Sean Baylor wasn't a solo act, Chili. He had a partner."

NOTES TO SELF

Although Chili's parents were as warm and supportive as always, I couldn't wait to go home. The group known as Baylor wasn't just Sean. It was Sean and a drummer. Once we left, I badgered my dad with questions. He promised to try to find a way to play the "LP," as he called it. I didn't have much hope in that department. Although he is the most creative person I know, my dad has been known to short out our electricity while trying to repair a table lamp. It's all right, though. I will find a way to listen to Sean Baylor's music. In the meantime, I am going to start seriously looking for the drummer.

There can't be that many people with the name of Eldon "Cookie" Burke. I might as well start by figuring out his sign.

14

The Fixed Scorpio wallows in those endless emotional waters more than most signs (except perhaps fellow Water signs, Pisces and Cancer). And it works, most of the time, at least. Although a person born under this sign might not be any more long-suffering than anyone else, you won't convince the Scorpio of that. Don't bother trying. It's a small price to pay for friendship with this eternally loyal comrade who will keep your every secret.

—*Fearless Astrology*

I didn't have to go far. Cookie Burke's birth date was on the first Web site I checked. He was born on November 2. A Scorpio. From the description in *Fearless*, it wouldn't be easy prying information out of him.

His career, although far less dramatic than Sean Baylor's, had lasted much longer. He and Baylor had started out in a folk band called The Twa Corbies, named after some Scottish ballad. I remembered from Ms. Snider's English class that *corbies* meant ravens or crows. And *twa*, as far as I could tell, meant *two*. Then Baylor's star had begun to rise, and the duo's name had changed to simply Baylor. Now, Cookie Burke was listed as, "Jazz man," on the Internet. "Home base, Monterey."

I shivered when I read that. Once class was over on Monday, I was going to look for this guy.

As usual, Candice had a party going on in our room that Sunday when I returned. She and the *out-of-staters*, as they had started calling themselves, had remained on campus and partied all weekend. I wondered if that included Jeremy. At least, he wasn't in the room that night. Vanessa was.

When Chili, Paige, and I walked in, she stalked out as if we were the ones invading her space.

"Who's the chest?" Chili asked.

Tati had been more than happy to fill her in.

Monday morning, Tati and I sat next to each other in class, as I wondered how I was going to find Cookie. From the back of the room, Jeremy gave me that same dark stare he had after Chili had yanked me away from him on Friday. He was dressed like an East Coast kid, all in black. Remembering the scene with Chili seemed strangely funny, and I had to look down to hide my smile and keep from laughing.

"*Ghost Seekers* will be here next week," Jaffa said and pulled his dorky scarf closer around his neck. "Today, I want to hear what you wrote, based on Friday's interviews. And I also want to know what progress you've made on your research."

"I had a terrible time, Henry." Vanessa sat straight in her chair as if to emphasize her seriousness. "I mean, astrology is just so dull, and those sites online are all the same."

"And her problem *is*?" Tati whispered. "She probably thinks research is supposed to be like flipping channels."

"Tatiyana." Jaffa said her name the way a judge in a court-room might, just before delivering a guilty verdict. "Do you have something to add?"

She shot him an innocent look and pushed back the hair that had fallen over one eye. "I've heard it said that there are no boring topics." Only boring researchers. She wouldn't dare say that. "When that happens in my own research, I try to challenge myself, and if I learn one new fact from any source, I consider it worthwhile."

"Excellent." She had won him over again, and Vanessa was clearly fuming.

"I did challenge myself." Vanessa tilted her head and glanced from Jaffa to me. "I helped Jeremy research Sean Baylor last weekend."

I turned. Now Jeremy was the one looking down.

"How did you do that?" I blurted without thinking.

"Oh," she said, and waved a hand in little circles as if illustrating their journey. "We went to a bunch of the places where Baylor had played, and I tried to conjure his spirit."

What I could see of Jeremy's face through the hair that was hiding it was a deep shade of red. *Good.*

"That's great," I said. "I did some Baylor research of my own."

"Really?" Her smile was superior. "I thought you just went home."

I hoped that Jeremy could hear the nastiness in her tone. If this was what he wanted, he could have her.

"Yes, I did." I looked at Jaffa as I answered the question. "I was certain I could locate a Baylor recording there, and I did."

"You did?" Jeremy's voice from the back. I didn't turn around.

"You found a recording?" Jaffa asked. "You see, class. She didn't have to go on the Internet, although I'm sure she did that as well. She went beyond that and found the real thing."

"I can't wait to play it," I said. "It was recorded live at the Monterey Pop Festival in 1967."

Jaffa continued questioning everyone, and I knew that I had impressed him. I also knew that I had delivered an unexpected blow to Jeremy's smug existence.

After class, I walked slowly out of the room and guessed that he would soon catch up with me.

He didn't waste any time. "Where did you find the record-ing?" he asked me.

I kept walking. "Just doing research, the same as you and Vanessa did."

"Logan," he said. "It wasn't like that."

I took my cell phone out of my backpack and checked for text messages. One from Chili. I needed to reply.

"See you later," I told him. "Good luck with your research."

I had already located the club where Cookie still played. I took a cab and got there early.

"ID?" squawked the sequined blonde at the entrance.

"I'm here for dinner," I said.

"This is still a nightclub, dinner or not. I can't let you in without ID."

Just then I caught the eye of an older guy. He was dressed formally in dark slacks and a long-sleeved shirt in a deep sapphire shade. The Afro had been trimmed and also light-ened by an invasion of gray. But the large, expressive eyes were the same.

"Cookie?" I asked.

"Hey." He nodded without smiling. "How'd you know me?"

"Your album. My dad has the LP, and I really just wanted to watch you perform."

"Let the kid in, Bernie."

"Whatever," the blonde said. "If there's trouble, it's on you, Cookie."

It was a small place. A tiny bandstand with a gleaming piano was at the back of the room, and dark red booths lined each side. The lights were too dim for me to see much more. Only a few people sat at the round tables in front of the bandstand.

I followed him inside, where he settled into a booth behind a candlelit table that held only a short glass with the remains of a drink in it.

"May I join you?" I asked. "It will just take a minute."

"Hey, I got you in the front door. What else do you want?"

"Just to talk to you about Sean Baylor."

"Forget it." He shook his head. "There's already way too much stuff about him going around right now."

"In a way, I'm part of that stuff."

He gave a sigh that could have been disgust or weariness, maybe both. "Okay, okay. Sit down. Want a Shirley Temple?"

"Water will be fine."

He motioned for the waitress, and I noticed that the ring on his right hand had a stone the same color as his shirt. "Water for the kid and another one of these for me, Bernie." Then he returned his attention to me. "So, how are you involved, and what are you doing here, anyway?"

"I'm looking for information about Sean Baylor," I said, "and I'm not going to lie to you. It's an assignment for Writers Camp."

"Everything you're hearing, all this ghost stuff, it's a crock. If you had anything to do with spreading it, you should be ashamed."

Our drinks came, make that his drink. He toyed with the

glass, kind of flirting with it. Watching him, I could almost feel his thirst; I could almost taste it. Scorpio was a Water sign, and water took the easiest way, the path of least resistance. I wondered if he was drinking to forget, or maybe just drinking to cope with this night in a less-than-crowded club.

"I didn't have anything to do with spreading the story," I told him. *Not yet.* "I was at the restaurant when we heard the music, and one other time on the beach."

He picked up the drink he had been eyeing. He sipped, swallowed, and smacked his lips. "I don't know what you did hear, but I can tell you what you didn't."

I noticed a slight slur in his voice and hoped the alcohol would loosen him up.

"Would it be okay if I do have that Shirley Temple?" I asked him. "You look about ready for another one too."

"Might as well," he said, and finished his drink. "Then I've got to go on."

"Do you perform any of the songs you sang at the festival?"

"No one wants to hear me do the Baylor stuff now." His voice cracked with what I guessed was supposed to be laughter. "Sean B. was the star. If it hadn't been for him . . ." He stopped and called out, "Hey, Bernie. A Shirley Temple and one more of these." I wondered what he was going to say. That Sean Baylor was the only reason that he got within inches of stardom? That Baylor's death triggered the descent that had landed him in a string of places like this?

"You were saying?" I asked.

"I don't remember, and it doesn't matter anyway. Sean B. would be the last person to haunt this town."

Bernie delivered the drinks. This time Cookie didn't flirt with his. He just tossed it back.

"How did he die?" I asked. "Do you think he was murdered?"

"Let's not go there, okay? I don't know any more than anyone else about what happened."

"But you had played together at the festival. Was he arguing with anybody, a woman maybe?"

"Yeah, maybe. There were always women, and so there were always arguments."

"Did he have a special one?"

He stared into his empty glass. "They were all special for as long as it lasted. You'll understand that someday if you ever fall for a musician."

My flesh went cold. There was no way he could know about Jeremy, but still that street-smart cynicism and those weary eyes sent a shiver through me.

The blonde approached our table again. "Another one, Cookie? You have time."

He glanced at me. "Go ahead," I told him. "I'm fine." Encouraging him to drink was not my greatest moment. Jaffa had warned us about six-pack journalism, as he called it. I rationalized by telling myself that this was Cookie's nightly habit. All that had changed was that I was here trying to get information out of a tight-lipped Scorpio. Tight-lipped until it came to those little shot glasses, that is.

"Do you remember who Sean was seeing at the time?"
I asked.

"No, and it wouldn't matter anyway. Bottom line, I just
think he made a bad decision. Lots of things can happen on
a sailboat at night."

"Did he go there alone?"

"I don't remember. Like I said, there were always fights
when women were around."

"What was her name?"

He shrugged. "Your guess is as good as mine."

I knew it.

"And they fought because of another woman, maybe?"

"Women, plural. Kid, you've got some imagination. Don't
be writing about any of this. My official story is that Sean B.
left alone for the boat."

This meant that he hadn't.

Bernie arrived again and slid another glass toward Cookie,
then discreetly removed the empty ones.

"Was there anyone who would have benefitted from his
death?" I asked.

"How the hell should I know? I don't even care how he
died anymore."

"Why are you so certain that his spirit isn't the one people
have heard at the restaurant?"

"I told you. It's a crock." He downed his drink with the
ease of someone who had been doing it for a very long time.
"Sean B. was like my brother, okay? He's dead, all right, but

he's no ghost. If he was, he'd be trying to find me or Ren, not a bunch of strangers in a restaurant."

"Who's Ren?"

"You're pretty good." He lifted his head, and for the first time, looked at me with respect. "She's his sister. Now, I really do have to get ready to go on."

"So where is Ren now?" I asked.

"Doesn't matter. You're welcome to stick around, but I'm finished answering questions."

"Do you think she would be willing to talk to me? I'd like to interview her."

"Kid," he said, "she won't even talk to me."

NOTES TO SELF

Cookie's fondness for what my gram would call drowning his sorrows is Water sign all the way. Unhappy Water sign, that is. It's clear to me that he's dealing with guilt issues. His best friend died. He's still around but nowhere close to where he might be if Sean had lived. And the way he dismissed the women! Sean Baylor had to have had a woman in his life. If he was a true Gemini, he was in love with being in love.

Cookie let me stay around because, he said, they needed to "fill the room." It wasn't very full, but he was so good that I wished I could just enjoy his music and not worry about what I have to do next. And what I have to do next, of course, is figure out a way to talk to Baylor's sister. I wonder what sign she is.

15

BE PREPARED WHEN DEALING WITH THE SIGN OF
CANCER. ALTHOUGH SOME CANCERS DEAL WITH THEIR
EMOTIONS, MANY CARRY HEAVY BAGGAGE, ENOUGH
THAT THEY CAN MAKE THEIR WATER SIBLINGS, SCORPIO
AND PISCES, APPEAR IN CONTROL AND ALMOST
ASSERTIVE BY COMPARISON. CANCER, ALTHOUGH OFTEN
AS PASSIVE AGGRESSIVE AS THE OTHER WATER SIGNS,
CAN ALSO BE DANGEROUS. THESE CRABS ARE
EXTREMELY PROTECTIVE, AND MANY HAVE MOTHER
ISSUES. THREATEN ONE OF THEIR OWN, AND YOU'LL BE
TAKING YOUR LIFE—LITERALLY—IN YOUR HANDS.

—Fearless Astrology

inding Ren Baylor online was easier than I had thought it was going to be. In addition to sitting on several nonprofit boards, she headed the Baylor Foundation for the Creative Arts. Her birth date was June 28. Cancer. Was she donating money to the arts in memory of her brother, or was she motivated by some other emotion? I would find out as soon as I could figure out a way to talk to her.

When I saw Jeremy in class that Tuesday, he gave me a look that wasn't as much nasty as disinterested. And disinterested hurt a little more than nasty would have. I remembered how terrible he had been to me. He, who had suggested that I was playing Baylor tunes on the beach, and who knew where else? He, who might have been "researching" with Vanessa over the weekend. I wanted to tell him about Cookie, but, since we weren't exactly speaking, I wouldn't be able to, not today, at least. There was still that little matter of his weekend research with Vanessa to discuss.

We'd barely gotten started when Jaffa called me to the front.

"I don't know what this is all about," he said, "but they need to see you in the admin office."

"Why?"

"I don't know. Get back as soon as you can. These administration people have no business interrupting my workshop."

I found my way to the right office.

"Your name?" the clerk inside asked.

"Logan McRae."

"She's the one."

I looked in the direction of the harsh voice and spotted a tall woman in a rust-colored coat about the same color as her sleek bob.

"You can go with Ms. Baylor." The clerk pointed toward an open office door.

I nearly stopped breathing. This woman in front of me must be Sean Baylor's sister. As much as I had wanted to find her, I wasn't sure how I felt about her finding me.

"You spoke with Cookie Burke last night?" she asked, and I knew he'd told her.

"Yes," I said, "and I'd like to talk to you."

"Fine." She turned her back on me and swept into the room.

I followed. *Sean Baylor's sister.* I couldn't believe my luck. Or was it my *bad* luck?

Once inside, she closed the door and sat at the head of a long table. I thought about it, okay, mulled it, and decided to sit at the other end. When I did, I really saw her for the first time.

She had one of those sharp, thin faces that would always be able to pass for pretty, regardless of her age.

"So, Ms. McRae," she said. "I understand you've been asking questions about my late brother."

"A lot of people have," I told her.

"But none of them has thought to trace the connection to Cookie Burke. My compliments."

"Cookie told you I was there?"

"How I found out is of no concern. All that matters is that

the questions you are asking about my brother are causing me a great deal of pain."

"That's not my intention," I said.

"His death destroyed our family right along with his promising musical career, and it's hurtful to have anyone making a mockery of all that." She cleared her throat and nailed me with her pale-eyed gaze. "Let alone a naïve college student."

High school, but I wasn't about to correct her.

"That's not what I want to do. I'm just trying to figure out what really happened that night."

"He fell off the boat, of course."

"Cookie suggested he had an argument with a woman."

"Don't trust him. He used Seanie too, like all the rest of his so-called musician friends." For a moment, I thought she might burst into tears, but she was far too controlled for that. "Cookie was the worst."

"So he wasn't the one who told you that I came to see him?"

She shook her head. "Stop asking pointless questions. All that does matter to me—and it matters very much—is that you will no longer contribute, in any way, to the gossip about my brother."

"This is not about gossip," I said. "I'm sorry you had to get involved."

"How could I not be?" Her voice caught. "I live this every day. I see his clothes, his car, his sailboat. I just cannot bear another reminder."

"Meaning?" I asked.

"Meaning that if you don't stop whatever it is you think you are doing, I will talk to the school administrators. You know what will happen then, don't you? The Baylor Foundation finances all of the arts programs here."

In spite of her martyred expression, I knew that I had never encountered such a dangerous enemy. Next to Ren Baylor, Vanessa was a minor irritation.

"How did you get in here anyway?" I asked. "Isn't it against the rules to take a student out of class?"

"Whose rules? I donate a great deal, ask for nothing in return, and am welcome, indeed admired here." Her thin lips curved into a smile. "Not that I need to explain myself to you. I believe the clerk had the mistaken impression that we were already acquainted."

So she had faked that. "I still can't believe they just had me taken out of Jaffa's workshop," I said. "What did you tell them when they asked you why you wanted to talk to me?"

That dismissive sigh again, as if I was unworthy of a response. "Nobody asked."

"Well, I think I'd better get back now. Jaffa isn't going to be happy about this." I met her eyes and made sure she got the message I didn't have the nerve to speak. *And I will tell him.*

"Don't cross me, Ms. McRae." She rose from her chair. "If you even attempt to continue this nonsense, you will find out what I'm capable of."

And with that final threat, she stalked out of the room.

NOTES TO SELF

Jaffa wasn't happy that I returned to class so late. If only my Mars in reluctant Pisces hadn't held me back from telling Ren Baylor that she couldn't stop me. I know that she will attempt to get me kicked out if she thinks I am going to stir up unhappy memories for her. Yet, I have no choice. If I am going to have Henry Jaffa for a mentor, I have to deliver on my Sean Baylor story. And it has to be a better one than Jeremy is going to turn in. It certainly has to be better than Vanessa's fake one on astrology.

16

IN MANY OF LIFE'S CHALLENGING MOMENTS, WE MUST
JOIN FORCES WITH THOSE WHO ARE THE MOST UNLIKE
US. FIRE MUST TEAM WITH AIR. AND EARTH WITH
WATER. GET THE IDEA? WE ARE ALL CONNECTED, AND
IN DIFFICULT TIMES, WE MUST MAKE THOSE CONNEC-
TIONS WORK.

—*Fearless Astrology*

*F*earless Astrology made sense, as it almost always
did. I was willing to team up with anyone if I must. If it
would help me unravel the mystery of Sean Baylor. And if it
would help me land Henry Jaffa for a mentor. I couldn't stick
around in the room tonight, though. Candice was having a
barbecue on our patio. I decided to skip it and go for a walk
to think about what to do next.

I left the dorms late that afternoon, glad that it wasn't as cold as it had been. My yellow hoodie should be enough to protect me from the weather.

"Logan, wait."

Jeremy stood just outside the building. He was still dressed in his East Coast clothes. I didn't know whether I should run to or away from him. This Aquarius had already learned the painful lesson of Jeremy charm. Might as well just pretend to be friendly.

"Hey," I said. "What are you doing here?"

"Looking for you. I was hoping you might be looking for me, too."

I didn't want to think about whether or not he was right. And I certainly didn't want to deal with the challenge in those sexy blue eyes. I didn't want to remind him that he had accused me of faking Baylor music. "Actually," I said. "I just needed a break."

"I get that. Am I wrong, or is there always a party going on in your room?"

"Mostly right. Candice is cool, so of course everyone wants to be around her."

"So would you like to take a drive?"

"What?" *Where had that come from?*

"Dirk's going to the barbecue, and I have his car again. I thought maybe we could check out 17-Mile Drive. Do some research."

"How did you and Vanessa happen to miss that last weekend?"

"Don't," he said. "She only talks that way to upset you. Dirk's the one she likes."

"But he's into Tati."

"Let's just say that Dirk has a problem making up his mind." He gave me that look he had the first night when he had reached out and grabbed me. "I'm not that way." *Taurus*, I thought. *Loyal.*

"So you weren't doing research with Vanessa?"

"Not the way she tried to make it sound, and I don't think I need to explain myself. Sean Baylor once owned a home on 17-Mile Drive. I'm heading over there. Why don't you come with me?"

No harm. If we could find where Baylor had lived, it would make up for Jeremy's nasty remark about not having to explain what he was doing with Vanessa.

At the end of Cannery Row, we passed the Monterey Bay Aquarium and began our drive around the peninsula. Ocean View Boulevard stretched out next to the Pacific. The view was more amazing with Jeremy than it had been in the past.

"I heard about what happened with Baylor's sister today," he said. "What did she have to say?"

The Taurus wasn't even looking at the magnificent view.

"How did you find that out?"

"Everyone's talking about it."

"Meaning Vanessa?"

That got him angry again. "So, you think she's my only source of information? I know that Baylor's sister was at school making all kinds of demands. What I don't know is why she picked on you."

I smiled into his face with a rush of confidence. "I'll tell you if you tell me."

"What's that supposed to mean?"

He pulled up to the pay booth at Pacific Road Gate and handed some bills through the window. The road swept around a bay, through the woods, and past homes that looked both unattainable and as down-to-earth as their natural surroundings.

"Well?" he asked.

"You know that I found a Baylor record last weekend. What I didn't say is that Sean Baylor wasn't a solo act. He had a partner. I managed to find the guy, and the word got back to Baylor's sister. She made some pretty nasty threats."

"Wow." He looked stunned, not in a drugged Critter way, but like a guy who was just realizing that his link to Baylor's family had been right in front of him all of the time.

We passed golf courses and country clubs, and then, some of the oldest Monterey cypresses in the world. Ahead of us, apparently blooming out of a garden of rocks, was the Lone Cypress Tree.

"Look at that," I said. "It's been around about two hundred fifty-something years, clinging to those rocks and surviving."

"You want to stop?"

The tiny parking lot was full of visitors, and the sky was deepening, more indigo now than blue.

"Maybe another time."

He turned and gave me the look again. "Is that a promise?"

"I wish it could be, but considering the length of our workshop, I can't promise much."

"Sure you can," he said. "My mom and I talked last night. I'm not going to school in New Jersey. I want to live in California. Here, actually."

"Oh." I could barely catch my breath.

He pretended not to notice. "I know we've had problems, Logan, but would you consider working together now?"

The question I'd been dying to hear, and there it was.

"Maybe," I said. "If you tell me what you're really doing here and why you're so interested in him."

"I told you. I'm here because of my music."

"And you really do think getting your article published is going to help your music career?"

"I know so." He reached out his hand again, and I took it even though I knew I shouldn't. "Please let's work together."

"Meaning tell you what Baylor's sister told me?"

"For starters."

"Not much. She was really nasty and condescending. A Cancer."

"Which means?" His voice still held some challenge, but not as much as before. And his fingers laced in mine were warm.

"Deep emotions, and maybe some mother issues. Loyal to the death when it comes to family." Then it hit me. "Jeremy, she's the one living in Sean Baylor's house on this drive. A

Cancer would never break those ties to family."

"So when we find the house, we find Baylor's sister?" he asked.

"Yes, we will, but I'm guessing it's inside one of those gated communities. Ren said that she kept all of his clothes, his car, and his sailboat."

"The sailboat," he said. "We've got to find it."

I let go of his hand, and missed the warmth the moment I did so. "Tell me the truth. Are you serious about working together? You're not going to accuse me of faking Baylor's ghost anymore?"

"I did that because you were on the attack. Help me find that boat, and I promise you we'll work as a team from now on."

I'd have to be out of my mind to trust him after everything he had pulled.

"Let's go," I said.

NOTES TO SELF

Yes, I have really agreed to do this. Yes, I am sitting here beside Jeremy in the car, windows down, smelling the ocean air. And, yes, looking at him, that perfect profile. He's staring ahead, intent on getting us to the pier. Maybe I can take one little sneak peek at *Fearless Astrology*. How am I going to figure out how to find the boat *Sean's Song*?

17

FUNNY THING ABOUT TAURUS. THE BULL CAN RAGE ALL DAY. HE CAN ACCUSE YOU OF EVERY CRIME. BUT THE FIRST TIME ANYONE THREATENS YOU, JUST TELL THAT TAURUS, AND IT WILL BE HANDLED, REGARDLESS OF YOUR SIGN. TAURUS IS THE GREAT PROTECTOR.

—*Fearless Astrology*

Baylor's sailboat had to be out here somewhere. It was definitely a long-term tenant, maybe the longest term of all. Once past the gate, I began scanning the sides of the boats.

Then I spotted it—much smaller than I'd imagined, its sail wrapped in a dark green fabric. *Sean's Song.*

"Is that it?" Jeremy asked.

"I think so."

"How do we know for sure?"

"The name," I said.

He turned to look, nearly tripped. Just then, I was the one hanging on.

"*Sean's Song*." He could barely speak. "You found it, Logan."

He scrambled aboard, and the boat rocked in the water. I was so cold, so scared that my teeth were chattering.

He lifted down a hand. I grabbed it and let him help me aboard.

Insane, absolutely insane. We were on Sean Baylor's boat. Right now, Sean Baylor's dipping up-and-down boat. My queasy stomach posed a question. I answered it with a single thought. *Later*.

Jeremy turned on a light and was already going below. I could only follow.

The first thing I saw was a small stove and other kitchen stuff to my right. *Galley*. That's what they called boat kitchens, wasn't it? Jeremy had already moved past it and the sofa tables on the left. I followed again, and found him in the boat bedroom—couldn't remember the word for that. He sat on the edge of the bed and rifled through papers that he must have yanked out of a net attached to the side.

"What are you looking for?" I asked.

"Not sure." He lifted a bulky envelope, and some photographs slid to the floor.

I picked it up. Sean Baylor and a dark-haired woman stood in front of the boat. With his arm around her, Baylor grinned at the camera. She glared at him and crossed her arms. Her dress was long and gauzy. His shirt was black, covered with a tiny purple print. Flowers.

"Baylor," I said. "He's wearing the same shirt he was on the cover of that Monterey Festival album."

"He probably wore it more than once." Jeremy was obviously pretending to stay rational. "Still, this could have been taken that night."

Another photo showed the same woman, her hand in front of her face.

"Look," I said. "She's not very happy. And look at all of the people behind them. It must have been at the festival."

"Who's in there?" A man's voice boomed from below the boat. I looked around wildly. No place to hide.

"Run." Jeremy dropped the envelope. "Meet me at the car."

Just as we cleared the galley, a large guy in a navy watch cap started to come aboard. A gold stud gleamed from his ear, and he held a lit cigarette.

"What the hell do you think you're doing?" He tossed his cigarette into the water.

Jeremy dodged him and scrambled over the side of the boat just as the man was coming up. They rolled to the deck, and the watch cap fell off.

I followed them, shouting. "No. Leave him alone."

"Run," Jeremy told me. "Get out of here."

"Help," I screamed, completely terrified now. "Someone, help."

Lights flashed on in the boats around us. "What's going on?" a deep male voice called out.

"Help us. This man . . ." Before I could finish, the guy had jumped off and was running down the deck.

Jeremy rose unsteadily to his feet, and I rushed to him. "Are you all right?"

He nodded. "The photos. I've got to go back for them."

"You can't. That guy would have killed you. Besides . . ." I showed him what I was holding. "I got one of them."

"Hey." Another man's voice.

Jeremy pulled me to him, and I shoved the photo in my pocket.

"It's okay." I could see him now. He must be the one who'd scared Jeremy's attacker away. He wore jeans and a gray short-sleeved T-shirt, in spite of the weather. As he came closer, I could see that he wasn't much older than we were, and that there was a girl with him.

"Are you kids all right?" he asked.

"Thanks to you," I said. "I'm Logan, and this is . . ."

"Did you see the guy who attacked us?" Jeremy interrupted.

They shook their heads. "We weren't paying any attention," the guy said. "It's a good thing you screamed. What were you doing out here anyway?"

I took a deep breath and headed for the nearest lie. "We got lost."

"Yes, lost," Jeremy echoed. "Looking for 17-Mile Drive. But we know where we are now. Thanks for your help."

"Sure thing." He put his arm around the woman's waist. "You shouldn't be around this boat so late, though. It's not safe."

"Why not?" I asked.

"That boat?" He pointed at *Sean's Song.* "It's supposed to be haunted."

"How do you know that?" I said.

"Nothing's happened exactly. Just weird lights at odd hours, and for the last couple of weeks, some music late at night. Be careful, okay?"

Then they turned and walked back the way they had come.

"We'd better get out of here," I told Jeremy. Then I realized that he was watching me in a weird way, the light making his pale eyes look like shadows. "What is it?" I asked.

"You didn't leave. I told you to run, and you didn't go."

"I couldn't."

We stared at each other for a moment. My mouth was completely dry, my heart still pounding.

"Man." He shook his head. "Let's get out of here."

NOTES TO SELF

It was a pretty sane suggestion. Let's get out of here. Before the guy who nearly clobbered us came back again. Before we were caught somewhere we were not supposed to be. Still, I feel he was also trying to escape from what had become a very personal connection in a very short space. And how do I feel? Still mulling, I guess.

18

When you think about Mars, think about how you engage in conflict. If your Mars is in a peace-loving sign like Pisces, that can temper even a stormy Aries Sun. If your Mars is in Scorpio, you'll stir dark, stagnant emotions into that caldron, even if your Sun sign is as bright as Leo. Stir in Libra instead, and you'll add Air-filled argument in place of emotion. Ask yourself how you feel about conflict, and you probably already know where your Mars resides.

—*Fearless Astrology*

Jaffa's Mars was in Libra. According to *Fearless*, that meant a calm exterior and a love for verbal sparring. It could also mean someone who could swing from one side of a debate to another, with winning the only goal. Unsure about how he would react to what happened yesterday, I decided to arrive early to class.

Yes, that was Vanessa's favorite kiss-up habit, but I was pretty sure she'd be distracted this morning by what had become an espresso ritual in our room. Since the weekend of the out-of-staters, Dirk, with his cool British accent, had become a regular. Vanessa had become much more friendly with Candice. I didn't mind that they had gone to the play downtown together, and I wouldn't have traded my evening—weird guy and all—to be there with them.

Sure enough, the classroom was empty. Except for Jaffa. He sat at the far table marking up what looked like one of his own books.

He lifted his head and nodded. "Come in, Logan." Then his expression grew more serious. "So, what happened yesterday to make you miss the first part of our class?"

"You mean no one told you?"

"I haven't asked," he said. "I wanted to hear it from you."

"It wasn't my fault. Sean Baylor's sister had them take me out."

"Why?"

"I'm not sure. Somehow, she found out that I was investigating her brother's death, and she told me I had to stop."

"That's unacceptable," he said. "She can't pull a student out of my workshop because she doesn't like the assignment

I gave. The woman doesn't have enough money to buy that kind of power."

"She did it. And she threatened me."

The door opened, and kids began to wander into the room. Tati was talking to Dirk. Vanessa's voice was louder than ever, but I could see she was watching the two of them with an angry little glint in her eye. The plunging sweater of the day was white, and she had tucked that long, black hair behind her ears. If the sparkling studs she was wearing were real, her parents must be as rich as Candice's.

Jeremy walked in last.

"Thanks for what you've shared with me," Jaffa lowered his voice. "I'll be speaking to the administrator. You don't have to fear that woman any longer."

"Thank you. I don't want to be a bother. I just . . ."

Before I could finish, the door opened again, and Ren Baylor swept in. Her auburn hair was pulled back so tightly that she couldn't grin if she had wanted to. And, believe me, she didn't. Beside her, was a bald guy in a suit, who reminded me of Dr. West, our vice principal at home.

"You." She pointed a finger at me.

"Hold on just a minute." Jaffa stood. "This is a private workshop. We do not appreciate anyone interrupting us in here."

"That girl tried to burglarize my sailboat," Ren said. "You're protecting a thief."

I glanced over at Jeremy. He gave a quick shake of his head.

"I didn't," I said.

"There's your answer," Jaffa told her. "And now, if you have no proof, please leave my classroom."

"Do you have any idea who you are talking to?"

"I might ask the same of you." He stared right back at her. "But I would hope that I'm less self-involved than that. Now, please leave this room right now, before I get really angry."

"Dr. Fletcher?" She glared at the man beside her.

"We need to discuss this back in my office," the man told her. "This isn't the same as a regular class. Sorry for the interruption, Mr. Jaffa."

"I can prove it," she said. "The security camera at the gate caught her coming through."

Jaffa ignored her. "Just escort the lady out," he told Fletcher. "If this happens again, I'll take the workshop elsewhere."

I could barely breathe for the rest of the class period. The security camera. Why hadn't I thought about that? Thank goodness, Jaffa didn't call on me. He said that our next assignment was the lead for our articles, and I wrote it down with shaking fingers.

Finally, class was over. I started for the door.

"Logan?"

I stopped. I turned slowly back to Jaffa's desk, unable to imagine what fate was in store for me.

Jeremy jerked his head and tried to tell me something with his eyes. Vanessa gawked. Tati and Candice looked confused. Slowly, everyone left the room.

"Sit, please." I pulled a chair up beside his. "Now," he said.

"Why did you lie?"

"I'm sorry." Tears filled my eyes, and I was so embarrassed that I wanted to run out of the room. "That woman, Sean Baylor's sister, said she'd have me thrown out of class, and she'd do it, too."

"Why did you go on that boat?"

"To look for clues about Baylor." Might as well spill what he had probably already figured out. "As I said earlier, when I was home last weekend, my dad gave me an old Sean Baylor record. It's called an LP."

"I'm familiar with them. Please go on."

"There was a photograph of Baylor's drummer on it, and I managed to find him."

"Here in Monterey?"

I nodded miserably. "Somehow, Baylor's sister found out that I had talked to Cookie, the drummer, and that's why she had me pulled out of class yesterday."

"And then you decided to investigate the boat?"

I nodded again. "But not to steal anything. My goal is to study Baylor from an astrological perspective. Although it may not seem that way, I'm very serious about writing, and all I want is a chance to learn from you."

His expression didn't change. "Who was with you last night?"

I paused, then muttered, "No one."

"Do you expect me to believe that you went out at night, alone, and went aboard that boat?"

Before I could answer, I heard a noise and looked up. Jeremy stood at the entrance of the room, his stance as arrogant as ever, shiny black hair covering his forehead.

"Did you forget something?" Jaffa asked him.

"Actually, I *remembered* something." He walked closer to where we sat. "I remembered that Logan would probably lie to protect me."

"Indeed."

Just what I needed. My face must be scarlet for sure.

"I'm the reason she was out there," Jeremy said. "I was the one who wanted to investigate Baylor's boat. So, if anyone's getting kicked out of this workshop . . ."

"No one's getting kicked out." Jaffa's voice was cold. "You kids took a big chance going out there alone. What if something had happened to you?"

"Something almost did," Jeremy said. "That's the other reason I came back here. When we were leaving last night, I was attacked by a guy who must have been hanging around outside. Logan screamed, and a couple came from one of the other boats. They scared the guy off."

"They told us that Baylor's boat is supposed to be haunted," I said, in a wavering voice. "The man who helped us said they hear music late at night."

"Really?" Jaffa stroked his chin. "This is an angle the *Ghost Seekers* people haven't even considered. You're planning to return, of course."

I shook my head, shocked at his response.

Jeremy nodded. "Of course," he said. "I found some photographs there."

"All right, then. What would you think about the three of us going there together?"

"You'd do that?" I asked. "With us?"

"Absolutely. As long as you're with me, I'll be responsible for your well-being, and I'm fine with that."

"Your *black belt* against the spirit world?" Jeremy asked.

"My *everything* against whatever is on that boat." Jaffa raised his voice just enough to make Jeremy look down. "So what do you say? Shall we schedule a little field trip tomorrow night?"

"Why not tonight?" Jeremy said.

"I have a conference call with my publisher, but I don't mind waiting a day."

"I'm going with you," I said.

"Good." He rose from his chair and gave me a dorky grin. "See how much better everything works when you tell the truth, Logan?"

NOTES TO SELF

Now Jaffa knows that I lied twice. I hate that. How am I going to get him for a mentor if he doesn't think he can trust me? Still, he wants to go back to the boat with us. If he thinks it's worth exploring, I'm okay with it, and Jeremy is more than okay. Tomorrow, we investigate *Sean's Song* again. This time with Jaffa's approval. This time with no scary guy. And this time with no Ren Baylor trying to get me kicked out of this workshop. Maybe then, I can gain Jaffa's respect.

19

WHEN CONFRONTING ADVERSITY, IT IS BEST TO RELY ON THE MOST ASSERTIVE PART OF YOUR SIGN. IF YOUR SUN IS PASSIVE OR ENTRENCHED IN EMOTION, FIND THE STRENGTH WITHIN YOU. DRAW ON THAT SPIRIT. SURE, IT WOULD BE EASY IF EACH OF US HAD A LOVING SUN SIGN, A MELLOW MOON AND VENUS, AND A MARS WITH THE FIRE OF ARIES, LEO, OR SAGITTARIUS. BUT MOST OF US DON'T. THAT MEANS THAT WHEN THE GOING GETS TOUGH, YOU MUST FIND THE STRENGTH IN YOUR CHART AND ACT ON IT.

—*Fearless Astrology*

WHERE'S YOUR MARS?

The placement of Mars can influence your Sun sign, just as your Moon does. Unlike your Sun and Moon, which define your basic personality, the placement of your Mars determines how you prefer to deal with conflict and how you go after what you want. Even what appear to be negative traits may actually be positive for your combination of planets. A peace-loving Pisces or conflict-fearing Libra, for instance, might be empowered by Mars in Aries.

Aries: *This is Mars' natural home, so if yours is here, that doubles and triples your warrior instinct. Conflict doesn't bother you. Sometimes you even go looking for it.*

Taurus: *With Mars here, you have a great need to succeed on your own terms and refuse to quit.*

Gemini: *This placement will make even the most timid Sun sign outspoken and opinionated.*

Cancer: *Mars' fire is diffused in this Water sign. In Cancer, Mars can make the coldest sign more protective, possessive, and sometimes capable of verbally exploding.*

Leo: *Mars in Leo can make the most passive sign push to get recognition and attention.*

Virgo: *Mars in Virgo can make even the sunny disposition of a Leo, Sagittarius, or Gemini turn critical and nitpicky.*

Libra: *Air expresses, and Mars here brings out any sign's desire to debate and win any argument.*

Scorpio: *With Mars in this sign, the most dispassionate* *signs are stirred by Scorpio emotions. This can work for or against you, depending on whether your emotional situation is positive or negative.*

Sagittarius: *With Mars in the ever-traveling, witty Sadge, even shy Cancers will be more verbal about what they want.*

Capricorn: *Mars in Capricorn will add a cool edge to event the most fiery Sun sign.*

Aquarius: *Strong opinions and radical viewpoints are often found in this combination. Mars in Aquarius also makes even a reclusive, shy Sun sign more social.*

Pisces: *This combination can be compassionate to others more than to self. With Mars in Pisces, there is a tendency to* daydream *rather than to* do, *which, unless checked, can stall or stop an otherwise promising future.*

Gram Janie was right again. I needed to ignore my mulling Sun and timid Moon and convince Jaffa that I was not a flake. Jeremy and I were supposed to meet him that night. And after class, I had an appointment with Mercedes, the reporter who had interviewed Baylor when he was still alive. Today, I would try extra hard to show how serious I was. And once the other students left, I was going to try to explain to him that I had only lied to keep Jeremy from getting in trouble. That was a good reason for lying, wasn't it? To keep from snitching on someone else? I hoped so, because I didn't want to face Jaffa tonight until the air was clear between us.

He was more stern than usual in class, and I wondered if it

was because he was still unhappy with me.

"Today, we're going to talk about the writer's voice," he told our group. "Who can define that for me?"

"It's the way you write, isn't it?" Vanessa said.

"Anyone else?" he asked in that way he did when the answer wasn't the one he was looking for.

No one else was stupid enough to take the bait.

"All right," he said. "Style is the way you write, and that can change. Tone is the way you sound, and that can change."

"How's that, Henry?" The girl had no shame.

"Can you tell her, Logan?" That shot me into panic mode, and I wondered if he was getting even with me for lying.

"Well, your tone might be humorous in one piece you write, and serious in another."

He nodded and continued staring at me. "And what is voice?"

"I guess it's what makes one person's writing different than anyone else's. It's . . . I'm not sure how to say it."

"Voice is *who you are*," he said, and I couldn't tell whether or not he had liked my answers. I definitely needed to apologize to him after class. "Your job as a writer is to uncover that voice. For starters, I want you all to write down one thing that you absolutely believe in."

I thought about it. What did I absolutely believe in?

"Candice?" he asked.

"My wonderful friends, and my guy at home, of course."

"Andrea?"

"My twin."

"Darla?"

Embarrassed smile. "*My* twin." Cancers, for sure. All about family.

"Christopher?"

Fuzzy-eyed gaze from Pisces Critter. "Being cool."

"Brad?"

Brad Dog rubbed a hand over his shaved head. "Getting published in the magazine."

"Dirk?"

"This girl I know back in London."

Now, that was a surprise. Tati and Vanessa both jerked around to look at him, as if thinking they should be the reason.

"Mariah?"

"Becoming a writer."

"Logan?" he asked.

"Truth, I guess."

"Indeed?" I knew he was probably thinking that was pretty phony coming from someone who had just lied to him. "Jeremy?"

"Independence."

"Another fine answer. Tatiyana?"

She pushed her hand through her hair. "Roots, I guess." She laughed and tugged at a purple strand. "And not these."

"Vanessa?"

"Me," she said.

He squinted as if he hadn't heard. "And by that, you mean?"

"Me, Henry. I believe in myself more than anything or anyone."

"Thank you for clarifying, Vanessa." He turned to the rest of us. "Take that value, whatever it is, and write about it for the next ten minutes. When you do, you will begin to hear the sound of your own voice. No one will see it. This exercise is just for you."

THE SOUND OF MY OWN VOICE

I know the sound of my own voice. It's the sound I hear when I walk on the beach alone. It's what I barely remember from a dream, but I know without a doubt, that it is the truth. I started to say Truth with a capital T, but real truth doesn't need fancy, self-conscious formatting.

Also, I'm thinking that truth doesn't come with a The, as in The Truth. It might come with an A, as in A Truth. And my truth might be different from your truth. I am glad no one is going to read this, because I would look like a pathetic loser.

I do know that I am going to continue my search for the truth I began seeking that first day when Jaffa scattered our topics on the floor. Not just astrology anymore, but Baylor.

Is this the way I find my voice? By talking about what I can't begin to understand? Here's the only answer I can drum up at the moment.

Maybe.

We finished the exercise, and Jaffa told us to put our papers away.

"You should try every day to freewrite on subjects that matter to you," he said. "It will help you find your true voice, as well as to find out who you really are."

Vanessa raised her hand. "Isn't there an easier way Henry?"

"Nothing about writing is easy, I'm afraid."

"Then why do people do it?"

"Because we can't *not* do it."

The class laughed. Tati rolled her eyes at me, and Jeremy glared at nothing.

"Could I talk to you after class?" Vanessa asked.

"Of course." He turned to us. "Does anyone else have questions?"

All I wanted was a few minutes to apologize to him, and now Vanessa was going to hog all of his time. Jaffa gave me a curt nod as I walked past. We were going to meet tonight, and I knew where. But I still wanted to talk to him right now.

I lingered outside the door, hoping their exchange would be a brief one.

"So, Henry, I was wondering why I have to turn in an article."

To my horror, the upper window was cracked open, and Vanessa's voice floated right through it. I shouldn't eavesdrop, but I couldn't help myself.

"I'm not sure what you mean," he told her. "You were determined to be accepted to this workshop, in spite of the fact that you didn't have a referral from your school. I allowed it only because of my friendship with your father."

"But I didn't want to be here for just the writing. You know that."

"I told you, and I told your dad that I have no influence on the other matter. None."

If he ever spoke that harshly to me, I would have burst into tears.

"Well, can't you try, Henry? Since I came all this way?"

"I'm hoping you also came *all this way*, as you put it, to learn about writing. Although I must admit . . ."

"Henry, look!" she interrupted. "Someone's hiding outside the door, and the windows are wide open."

I tried to leave, but it was too late. In seconds she had rushed out and was throwing an Aries fit.

"What are you doing out here, Logan? What did you overhear?"

"Nothing, and calm down, will you? I was waiting for you to finish so that I could speak to Mr. Jaffa." This time I was telling the truth. I only hoped Jaffa could tell it.

"Vanessa was just leaving," he told me. "Let's go back inside."

"I am really leaving, not just pretending to," she shot back. "So, don't worry, Logan. I won't be sticking around to spy on you."

NOTES TO SELF

There are many lovely Aries people in the world, but Vanessa isn't one of them. Now, it makes sense why a ditz like her even got admitted here. Jaffa is friends with her dad. But why did she want in this workshop if she doesn't care about writing? What is she really after?

Once Jaffa and I returned to the room, I apologized to him for lying and telling him I was alone when I got onto the sailboat. He didn't say that he understood; he didn't even say that he forgave me. However, he did say he appreciated my "making the effort," whatever that means.

Tonight we do our own version of *Ghost Seekers*, and maybe we'll get a chance to bond. Right now, though, I need to find the one reporter who met Sean Baylor. But I do think I am beginning to find what Jaffa calls my voice. Maybe that's a start.

20

REGARDLESS OF HOW PASSIVE YOUR SIGN IS, DO NOT FEAR FIRE, WATER, AIR, EARTH. DO NOT FEAR. INSTEAD, INVESTIGATE AND EXPLORE. MAYBE EVEN RELISH THE DIFFERENCES BETWEEN YOURSELF AND OTHER, EVEN MORE AGGRESSIVE SIGNS.

—Fearless Astrology

ercedes Lloyd-Chambers wasn't at the newspaper, and my helpful security guard couldn't tell me when she would be.

"She comes and goes." He stepped into the elevator and spoke through the open door. "You'll probably find her on the beach down by Jack's Crab Shack. Long hair, and curly like yours."

"Thanks." Before I could ask more, the elevator door slid shut.

It was warmer than usual on the beach that afternoon, and not many people walked along the strip of sand by Jack's Crab Shack. I noticed the tall woman with the long gray hair streaming behind at once.

"Mercedes," I called out, and hurried to catch up.

She turned. "You're Logan, right?"

"Yes," I said. "I'm so glad to finally meet you."

"You're a pretty girl." She grinned at me. "Fabulous hair. Never let anyone talk you into straightening it." I had to laugh. My frizzy hair was almost as wild as hers. And this had to be the strangest greeting I had ever received.

"I'd love to straighten it," I said. "Bring on the flat iron."

"One day, you'll adore it." She raked her fingers through the gray mass that swirled around her head.

As I looked at her, I realized that she was an original. Although not one of her features would be described as beautiful, together they were striking.

"I appreciate you meeting me," I said and took out my notebook. "Sorry I'm late. I went to the newspaper first."

"Really? I left a message on your phone."

"I haven't had a chance to check. I just figured you'd be there."

"I retired several years ago," she said. "I still write an occasional column."

"But I saw your office."

"My former office," she corrected me. "I'm flattered that a lot of the old timers still think of it as mine. Now, why are you so interested in Sean Baylor?" She sat down at one of the tables outside of the Crab Shack, and I joined her, breathing in the smell of food.

"Because I'm working with Henry Jaffa at Writers Camp Monterey, and Baylor's my assignment."

"So you don't have a personal interest in Sean?"

Should I lie? No, not after what I'd just been through. I'd done enough of that. I wasn't very good at it, either.

"To be honest," I said, "I only heard of him after Henry Jaffa assigned me the topic. My dad did give me an LP of his, though."

"Sean Baylor is much more than a college class topic." Her expression seemed to cloud over, and I knew that I was losing points. "Why would Henry Jaffa want you to write about someone you don't even care about?"

"I didn't say I don't care about him," I told her. "I said I hadn't heard about him until I began studying with Jaffa."

"So you do care?"

"I'm intrigued." That was the truth, too. Why was I doubting my own honesty, all of a sudden? Even to myself.

"Intrigued, how?"

I realized that she had taken charge of the interview, but I didn't know what to do about it. "The ghost aspect," I said.

"I don't buy that. Do you?"

"I heard the music."

Her body seemed to freeze. Only her hair moved in the wind. "Did you really?"

I nodded. "Twice. Once in the hotel, and once when I was walking back from the beach to my dorm." I felt chills along my arm and remembered how terrified I had been. "It was probably the scariest thing that has ever happened to me."

"I just don't believe it," she said. "Perhaps your imagination . . ."

"No," I said. "I really did hear it."

"I like to think I have an open mind, okay? But if Sean's spirit was going to be anywhere, it wouldn't be at that restaurant or on a piece of beach he never walked when he was alive."

"Where would it be?"

"You're a good little interviewer." She almost smiled, but not quite. "It would be the fairgrounds, of course. That was his finest moment."

"At the Pop Festival?"

"Yes. It's difficult for someone your age to understand, but we were not much older than you are right now. Some of those kids who played at that festival became the most gifted musicians of our generation."

"I know," I said and tried to impress her with my research. "Simon and Garfunkel, Janis Joplin, Sean Baylor."

"All playing together." She looked down at her clasped hands on the table. "And too many of them died too young."

"And you believe that's where his spirit is?"

"If it is anywhere, yes."

"And not on the sailboat?"

She stiffened in her chair. "Why would you ask that?"

"Because when I went there, people who lived on one of the other boats said they had heard his music."

"The boat." She put her hand over her lips and squinted into the sun. Then she leaned across the table and stared into my eyes. "They really think he's there?"

"I don't know," I said. "That's just what the couple I met there told me." I was careful not to say the couple *we met*.

"The sister owns the boat now. Her name is Ren. She is not a nice person."

"I discovered that," I told her. "She doesn't want anyone asking questions or writing about Sean."

"Then that much hasn't changed. You seem like a nice kid, Logan, but I don't know how I can help you. Sean Baylor was a talented singer with very modest ambitions. If you quote me, I guess you could say that. The music came first with him, not the career."

I scribbled down her quote and asked, "What kind of person was he?"

"Brilliant." She looked right into my eyes again with such a fiery expression that I knew that she must be either Aries or Leo. "Generous, and yes, funny."

"Sounds like a nice guy."

"Maybe. I've heard that he could get very moody. Those who knew him said that Baylor could go from the sweetest guy in the world to a wild man if anything set him off."

"Textbook Gemini," I said.

She laughed. "You must have looked that up ahead of time."

"I did," I said. "I appreciate you meeting with me. Before you go, would you mind telling me something? I'd really like to know what you would do if you had been given my assignment. How would you investigate Sean Baylor, ghost or no ghost?"

"Good question," she said. "The fairgrounds."

Her voice held that same longing my dad's did when he talked about the countries he and my mom visited when they were first married. I felt a lump in my throat.

"Want to go with me?" I was so shocked that I'd asked the question that I had to look down at my notebook to hide the blush I felt spreading across my cheeks.

"No way. There are too many ghosts out there, and not the kind you're hoping to find. Don't go alone, though." She got up from the table. Her hair glinted silver in the sunlight. "Stay safe, will you? I need to move on now."

With her dress and her hair floating around her, she stepped away from me and down the beach. I watched her disappear into the fog so easily, that if I hadn't known better, she might have been a ghost herself.

NOTES TO SELF

I am starting to wonder if I will ever able to conduct a decent interview with anyone. Mercedes took charge the moment we started speaking. When I mentioned the boat, I could tell that she didn't want anything to do with me or it. Yet I will be on it again in a few hours. I wish I knew her sign. Perhaps I'll have time for a little library research before we go back to the boat tonight.

21

IT'S ALL RIGHT TO ASK FOR HELP. REMEMBER THIS, WHATEVER YOUR SIGN. THE WAY YOU ASK CHANGES WITH THE PERSON, HOWEVER. SOME SIGNS REALLY DO WANT TO HELP YOU FOR THE SAKE OF THAT ALONE. SOME WILL TURN YOUR REQUEST INTO A VEHICLE FOR THEIR OWN ISSUES. STILL OTHERS WILL WANT TO KNOW WHAT YOU CAN DO FOR THEM. BEFORE YOU ASK, ASSESS.

—Fearless Astrology

The cute Aries with the patent leather red streak in his black hair was working on his laptop when I arrived at the library. Fire signs could be pretty generous. Thus, I figured I should be direct in asking for his assistance.

"Hey," he said.

"I'm so glad you're here. I could use some help." Pretty

direct, at least I hoped it was.

He grinned. "What kind of help? The guy who checked out the Baylor books still hasn't returned them."

"I know," I said. "Actually, this time, I'm just looking for the birth date for Mercedes Lloyd-Chambers, a reporter from the newspaper here. She interviewed Sean Baylor, and I'm guessing she must have been at his Monterey concert."

"Let me check it out," he said. "The name's familiar, but I've only been here a couple of years."

He motioned back to a computer behind his wrap-around front desk. I followed. He keyed in information. I waited.

"Mercedes Lloyd," he said. "Close enough? She was born October twelfth. I have an image here."

I walked around behind his desk. There she was, all right. The wild gray hair was shiny black, and the pale eyes were bright and intriguing. Then I realized it wasn't just a photograph he was showing me. It was a photograph of an "LP" shot. Mercedes was the woman, along with the blondes, on the cover of the record my dad had given me. Mercedes not only knew Sean. She was friendly enough with either Cookie or him—or both of them—that she had shown up in the crowd of admirers on his album cover.

Then I remembered the photo that I had taken from the sailboat. The woman who had been with Sean Baylor—that angry, brunette, arms crossed. Mercedes.

"Can you find out anything else about her?" I asked.

"It might take some time. Drop by tomorrow, if you can,

and I'll give you whatever I dig up."

I met Jeremy outside the dorm, and we drove over to the pier in Dirk's car.

Other than a bored-sounding, "Hi," Jeremy said nothing else to me during our short drive. I noticed the way he looked, though. I couldn't think about that, because if I did, I would get hurt beyond anything I could imagine. He was that great looking, and that dangerous. Once this was over, I would tell him what I had found out about Mercedes.

Jaffa was waiting for us outside the gate, bundled up in a wool scarf, as usual. He waved, and we joined him.

"All right," he said. "We're avoiding the security camera this time. Let me go first."

"Because you have the black belt, and we don't?" Jeremy asked.

"Because I am responsible for you, in case you haven't figured that out yet. If one of you kids get hurt . . . well, let's not even go there."

"All right, then," Jeremy said. "Let's get going. I want to see the rest of those photos."

"Okay. You kids wait here. I'll tell you when it's safe."

He turned his back just as a large guy walked out of a haze of fog.

"It's him," I screamed. "He's the one who tried to fight Jeremy."

Jaffa jumped down beside me.

"You don't learn, do you?" the man told me. He smelled of

cigarette smoke. The stud in his ear glinted in the dim light.

"Wait a minute," Jaffa said. "How do you have the right to guard these boats?"

"It's my job. These vandals broke the law, and if you want them to stay healthy, you'd better keep them away from here. They caused all kinds of damage."

"That's a lie," I said. "We didn't touch anything."

"Let's all go aboard then," Jaffa told him. "I'd like to survey the damage."

"It's fixed now. We got it all cleaned up."

"We?" Jaffa asked. "So you work for the owner?"

"That's none of your business."

"If you won't tell us who you're working for, and you can't prove that you have a right to be here, I'm afraid I'll have to call the police."

"Try it, and you'll be sorry, old man." With that, he charged Jaffa. Not a good idea. With a single movement, Jaffa sent him flying to the deck. The man shook his head as if trying to ground himself, then pulled up to his feet.

"You crazy old coot. You can have the damned boat for all I care. Go out there and die the way Baylor did."

Jaffa took a step toward him, and he turned and walked so fast the way he'd come that he was almost jogging.

We stood speechless for a moment. I felt light-headed and giddy. Images of what might have happened filled my mind, and I forced myself to erase them. Jaffa had turned the whole horrible situation around. We were safe.

He adjusted his scarf and grinned at us. "So, how was I?"

Jeremy nodded. "You were all right."

"Logan?"

I threw my hands in the air and tried to imitate that Aries shriek. "Oh, Henry, you were wonderful."

Jeremy grinned and slammed his hand over his mouth.

Jaffa shrugged away my comment, the way he did Vanessa's crazy outbursts in class. "You must remind me to tell you about my college roommate one day, Logan. He helped me a great deal in any number of ways. But I think he and I are just about even now. Shall we go aboard?"

NOTES TO SELF

I am in bed and trying to calm down. Candice went out with Vanessa and the New York twins to the theater again, and I just put *Fearless* in its usual hiding place, under the pillow of the bottom bunk. I still can't stop my wild heartbeat. We could have been killed tonight, Jaffa for sure. How did that creep know we were going to be there, or does he patrol the place every night? Jaffa guessed that he might be a hired guard, which would mean that Ren Baylor is paying him to keep people away from the boat.

Once we were onboard, it was clear that guard guy

had lied about the damage we had supposedly caused. The boat looked just the way it had the night before. Jaffa was clearly disappointed that no spirits greeted us in the galley. I was relieved that I didn't have to hear that eerie song again. Jeremy disappeared into the back area, and I knew he was after the photographs. He came back with an envelope, but other than a few at the festival, they seemed to be only family photos of Sean and Ren. Tomorrow night, I'm going to see Cookie again. First I have to suffer through another class with Vanessa. At least it makes sense now. Her dad was Henry Jaffa's college roommate. But as he said, that debt is nearly paid off.

22

Betrayal from someone you trusted provokes different reactions in each sign. Fire signs (Aries, Leo, and Sagittarius) fly into a rage. Earth signs (Taurus, Virgo, and Capricorn) hang on. They will try to work it out because they hate change. Air signs (Gemini, Libra, and Aquarius) get even. Water signs (Cancer, Scorpio, and Pisces) try to ignore betrayal (or any problem) as long as possible. Remember that the problem will not be found in your sign but in that of the betrayer.

—*Fearless Astrology*

anessa was not really my competition. She seemed more interested in hanging out at the theater than working on her writing. I remembered that her original topic had been about breaking into Broadway musicals, and with that Aries sun, she was more suited to that than facing a computer screen every day.

She wasn't my competition for Jeremy any longer either, if she ever had been. When he looked at me, his cocky expression became almost tender. I no longer believed he was faking an interest in me.

Back in class, we sat at our separate tables. Vanessa's sweater was gray, chaste, and pearl-buttoned to her chin. A new image? Not really. As I watched her take a seat at the table beside Candice, I noticed that, beneath that sweater, she was wearing a short skirt that slid up almost to her hips when she sat.

She was giving Dirk a fine view. He pulled up a chair across from her to take full advantage. Tati made eye contact with me and shook her head.

"Okay, people." Jaffa was still wearing the same navy scarf he'd worn when he'd taken on that guy last night. "I want to hear those leads today, and I want to hear the Baylor ones first. Can we start with you, Logan?"

Being first was almost a relief. I wondered if he knew that, then I looked down at the page in front of me and began to read.

Was all we had to say to each other
all we had to say to each other?
Was forever only a feeling . . .

"With these simple lyrics, folksinger Sean Baylor expressed the way that he defined love and desire in the late 1960s. To that Gemini male, love and desire were the same; and they were indeed interchangeable."

"How did he live? How did he love? How did he die? It's all in Sean Baylor's chart, something far more complex than the sixties question, 'What's your sign?'"

"Excellent, Logan," Jaffa said. "It offers promise and intrigue. Good job. Jeremy, would you like to go next?"

"Sure." He glanced down at the paper in front of him. "Sean Baylor's ghost is the stuff of legends. His music haunts a Monterey restaurant. Stories of his sightings abound. The sixties-era folk singer is believed to have drowned after taking out his sailboat following his show-stopping performance at the Monterey Pop Festival in 1967. But what if it's not Sean Baylor's ghost that haunts the beach? And what if his death was no accident?"

"I like it," Jaffa said. "It hooks the reader and makes him want to read more. You and Logan are using questions in your leads. Although they work in both your cases, they can be easy to overdo. Now, who would like to go next?"

"I will." Vanessa raised her hand. "It's not very long, and so not as wordy as the first two. But it is the essence of my article. It's a way of looking at fictional characters in astrological terms. And it has some questions in it too."

"That sounds very promising, Vanessa." Jaffa looked surprised. "Let's hear it."

"It's called, 'Hamlet Was a Libra,' and here's how it starts." She took a sip from her water bottle. "'To be or not to be?' With all of his wondering and all of his questioning, Hamlet had to be a Libra. They frequently have trouble making up their minds. His love for beauty—think Ophelia—is par for the course for one ruled by Venus. There's a lot of talk from this Air sign, too, and Libras are known for their communication skills."

I couldn't believe what I was hearing. She had stolen my words. Somehow, Vanessa had found my hidden astrology book and ripped off the first part of the Hamlet piece. Fortunately, that was all she had.

"Since you like the first part, what do you think about my argument that he could be other signs?" I asked her.

Her eyes went blank. She glanced from me to Jaffa. "What are you talking about? Hamlet was a Libra. That's my hook. It works, Henry, doesn't it?"

"It might," he said. "Logan, what are your thoughts?"

"My thoughts—the ones I didn't write down to be stolen— were that Hamlet could have been a Gemini or even a Sadge. And with all of that karmic family emotional stuff, he could have been a Scorpio or a Cancer, too."

"So, in this fictional astrological model, Hamlet may not

have been a Libra?" Jaffa asked. "Is that what you're trying to say?"

I shook my head and met his eyes. "What I'm trying to say is that Vanessa plagiarized the first paper I tried to write for this workshop. She flat stole it."

"That's ridiculous, Henry," Vanessa whined. "Who'd want to plagiarize someone as boring as Logan?"

"You would." My voice shook. "You did. And I have another question."

"What?" Jaffa asked.

Nothing to lose now. I might as well go for it. I'd been betrayed, and I knew it. Not only by Vanessa either. I stared at Candice, that long, shiny blond hair. Those dark eyes and straight, pale lips.

"Why?" I asked her.

She stood up, started to speak, then ran from the room.

"Candice was the only person who knew where my astrology book was hidden," I told Jaffa. "My notes were in it, and now, Vanessa is quoting my own words back to me."

"It's not true," Vanessa said. I could hear the buzz of doubt in the classroom. No wonder, considering the doubt that Jeremy had already cast. "Not true at all. I didn't try to steal that book. Candice offered it to me."

"No," I said.

"Oh, yes she did. I didn't even know the creepy old thing existed." She turned to Jaffa. "Henry, it wasn't my fault. Candice showed me where Logan had hidden the stupid book." My stomach turned with every word. "I didn't plagia-rize, either, exactly. Her idea about Hamlet being a Libra sounded okay, so I decided to write my article about that."

"Class." Jaffa stood. His voice was the deadly quiet one he had used when he spoke to the guy guarding the sailboat. "You are excused for the rest of the day. Vanessa, please come to the front."

"But Henry . . ." It was the last thing I heard her say.

When I got to the room, Candice was already packing her stuff into boxes. And she had a lot of stuff. I realized just then that the floral arrangements, crystal glasses, and china cups had all been hers. Not to mention that humongous coffee machine. There was barely a trace of me left in this room.

"I take it you're leaving," I said.

She pulled up her hair and twisted it to the back of her head. "Trading roommates. I can't wait to get out of here."

"I thought we were friends. Why did you turn on me?"

"Friends!" I realized that her serene expression was about as steady as a china cup on a narrow ledge. Never had I seen such a seemingly calm face mask such internal chaos. "You remind me of my sisters. You get all the attention in class. You can't decide between two guys, and the only person who cares about me is Vanessa."

"But what about your boyfriend at home?" I asked. She glared at me through her tears, and, just like that, I knew. "There isn't any boyfriend at home, is there?" And probably no wonderful friends either. So that's why she was throwing the 24/7 espresso fests and barbecues here. She was trying to buy herself the life she didn't have at home. I would feel sorry for her if she hadn't been so awful to me.

"I don't know your sisters," I said, "but for what it's worth, I liked you for who I thought you were. No one is going to really like you, though, not when you do the kind of things you did to me."

"Vanessa does," she said.

I didn't reply. Let the Virgo and the Aries figure it out for themselves.

NOTES TO SELF

True to my Air sign, I should want to get even, but that's not how I feel. I feel, well, betrayed. So, here I am, alone in the room. It still feels bizarre and unreal that Candice was jealous of me or that she told Vanessa where I had hidden *Fearless Astrology*. I'm better off knowing the truth about her. Wait. I hear a knock at the door. If it's Candice, I swear I'm not letting her in.

I get up. "Who is it?" I ask.

"Me, Tati."

I yank open the door, and she stands just outside with two suitcases as purple as the streak in her hair.

"Hey," I say. "Are you my new roommate?"

"Looks that way. Vanessa just kicked me out. Must be a lucky day for this Capricorn."

I put out my arms and hug her.

"Come on in," I say. "It's finally become a lucky day for this Aquarius, too."

23

THERE IS A TIME WHEN EVERY SIGN MUST DRAW STRENGTH FROM WITHIN. FIRE SIGNS DRAW IT FROM BELIEF IN THEMSELVES. EARTH SIGNS DRAW IT FROM BELIEF IN THEIR BELIEFS. AIR SIGNS DRAW IT FROM BELIEF IN THEIR WORDS. WATER SIGNS DRAW IT FROM BELIEF IN THEIR FEELINGS.

—Fearless Astrology

Air sign that I was, I knew that I needed to draw strength from my own words. I couldn't escape back home the way a Pisces, Cancer, or Scorpio might. Although it would be great to see Chili, Paige, and my dad, and maybe even Nathan (just to let him know that I no longer cared about him, right?), I needed to do something else this weekend. And that was to pay another visit to Cookie Burke. I had to warn him that Ren Baylor knew that we spoke, and even more important, I needed to ask him about Mercedes Lloyd-Chambers.

Saturday morning. Tati and I had herb tea on the patio. I must admit it was kind of nice waking up to peace and quiet and not the roar of an industrial strength, dressed-to-impress espresso machine. Kind of nice drinking from cheap mugs instead of heirloom china. The room seemed airier, less tense without Candice and her baggage in it.

Even though Tati and Candice were both Earth signs, I should have paid more attention to all of the emotional Water signs in the rest of Candice's chart. I should have also paid more attention to all of the nasty stuff she said about her sisters. Not to mention that fake-calm expression of hers that looked like glass on the brink of shattering.

I could only imagine the conversation Jaffa and Vanessa had shared yesterday. My guess was that whatever debt he had felt he owed his college roommate was paid off in full.

After we finished our tea, Tati went to meet Dirk, who apparently hadn't been entirely captivated by Vanessa's legs in class on Friday, after all.

And I went to meet Cookie Burke.

He'd been reluctant to talk again but finally agreed to meet me at a little chocolate shop on Cannery Row. If this place had a sign, it would have to be an Air sign. Everyone was chattering to each other and to strangers in other booths.

"Hey, kid. Over here." Cookie had been standing there all

along, but he looked different in the dark glasses and black leather jacket.

"Hi," I said. "I didn't recognize you."

"That's the idea. I didn't think anyone would notice us in here."

"So Ren Baylor got to you, too."

"She tried to get me fired from my gig. I've been playing at that club for years. It was a bummer having to ask the manager to go to bat for me."

"Why is Ren Baylor afraid of you?" I asked.

"Who knows? The woman doesn't want any publicity about her brother, but with all this *Ghost Seekers* stuff going on, she doesn't have a choice."

I took out my notebook. "Why you think Ren wants to stop the ghost stories?"

"Probably for the same reason I do, and it might be the only time she and I have agreed on anything in our lives. They're faked, and that's it in a nutshell."

"How do you know that?"

He took off his dark glasses, stared into my eyes with such emotion that if I hadn't already known he was a Water sign, I would have figured it out right then. "Because Sean Baylor was like my brother, that's how. Why would he be haunting some fancy restaurant? We lived on chow mein, pizza, and take-out chicken back then. If he was really some kind of ghost, he would be haunting me or the burger joint on the pier."

"What about the fairgrounds?"

"Maybe there. Assuming he's anywhere, that is, and I don't believe it." He looked off into the ocean. "The fairgrounds. Yeah, that's where we had one of our best times."

"*The Ghost Seekers* people are filming here next week. Do you think I should take them out there?"

"Who cares? The best thing that could happen is for the *Ghost Seekers* to go back where they came from, and for everyone else to stop talking about Sean."

I got the feeling that he was asking me to stop the publicity. "There's nothing I can do about it." I reached in my book bag and pulled out the record my dad had given me.

He took it, ran his long musician-fingers over the cover. "You shouldn't have brought it. Too many hard memories."

I touched the face of the wild-haired brunette smiling up at them. "Who's she?"

"Who knows after all these years? There were lots of women."

"You hinted that Sean had a special one, and that they argued the night of his death. I was just wondering if this might be the girl you were talking about."

"And I told you that you have some imagination. I can't tell you anything else. Just drop it." He turned the album over so that the photograph was facedown. "This whole Baylor mess needs to go away, but you just keep on stirring the pot."

I took out the photo I'd removed from the boat and put it on top of the album. "Her name was Mercedes, wasn't it?"

"Don't." His tone went cold.

"I talked to her," I said.

"You see what I mean?" He got up so fast that he almost knocked the table over. "You kids are poking around where you shouldn't. You can't seem to understand this is someone's life you're messing with."

"I do understand," I told him. "If you tell me the truth about Sean Baylor, I can write the real version, and we can stop all of the crazy *Ghost Seekers* stuff."

He stared at me for a moment, and I got that uneasy feeling again. "The truth, huh?" he said.

"Do you want Ren Baylor out of your hair or not?"

"Mercedes Lloyd. She was Sean's woman. They fought like hell the night he died. Write what you need to and don't bother me again."

As if disgusted with himself, me, or maybe both of us, he turned and walked out of the restaurant.

NOTES TO SELF

I'm so glad I stayed in town this weekend. Even though Cookie hadn't wanted to, he had confirmed what I had suspected. My brain is spinning out all kinds of possibilities. Did Mercedes murder Baylor? Did they fight on the boat, and did he fall overboard? I can't wait to hear what Jeremy thinks. I can't wait to see him. Lucky for me, he'll be here all weekend, too.

24

At some time in your study of astrology, you need to look at where your Venus is located. Venus is love, and where your Venus is will determine how you deal with your passionate relationships, and the other ones, too.

—Fearless Astrology

WHERE'S YOUR VENUS?

Aries: *Attractive, confident, sometimes arrogant. What you need from a partner is breathing room and spontaneity. You are Fire and may create sparks with Air signs Gemini, Libra, and Aquarius.*

Taurus: *Purposeful, sexy, loyal. You need a partner who will appreciate your sensuality and share your appreciation* *of the comforts of life. Earth and Water signs are a good start.*

Gemini: *Charming, eloquent, often opinionated. You need a partner who will calm your tendency to give up on a relationship too soon. Best bets are Fire and Air signs.*

Cancer: *Caring, moody, tied to mom or a mother figure. An urge to merge completely, especially with someone who reminds you of a lover from your past, or even the real thing. Best bets are a loyal Taurus, Scorpio, or Pisces.*

Leo: *Sexy, and fully capable of stealing the spotlight from just about anyone. You need a partner who is even more demanding, exciting, and in charge than you are. Best bets are those Air signs, Gemini and Libra. And maybe even a Fire sign or two.*

Virgo: *Observant, discriminating, eternally youthful. Earth signs such as Taurus and Capricorn will provide security and lessen what can be judgmental attitudes.*

Libra: *Diplomatic, uncertain, a need for attention and balance. Best bets include fellow Air signs Gemini and Aquarius, and sometimes even a little Fire. Aries, anyone?*

Scorpio: *Dark, emotional, passionate. You need someone who appreciates you for your ability to care about and keep secrets. Best bets are Water signs Cancer and Pisces.*

Sagittarius: *A need to get around, through travel and sometimes, various partners and interests. Judge your audience before you speak. Another Sadge will appreciate you for who you are. Other best bets are fellow Fire signs Aries and Leo.*

Capricorn: *Deliberate, organized, hard-working. Able to overcome most obstacles. Best bets include Fixed signs, especially Taurus and Virgo.*

Aquarius: *Faithful, distracted, committed to larger concerns. You refuse to be bored. Thus, your best bets are your own Air sign, including Air sign Gemini.*

Pisces: *Another emotional sign, lots of Water. If not careful, the last car of that zodiac train can not just take up the rear, but be a doormat. Go for an Earthy Taurus or Capricorn.*

Chili and Paige arrived on Saturday night, and they connected with Tati, as I knew they would. Waking up with my best friends and Tati in the same room that Sunday made me feel as if I were home. Before the others woke, I read about Venus and was surprised to see that Jeremy's Venus was in Cancer. Although I wouldn't have guessed it, I knew he was very close to his mom. That made sense. From what I could figure out, a loyal Fixed Taurus with his Venus in emotional Cancer might stick with the first female he falls for. Hmmm.

I could have sat there all day Sunday with Tati, Paige, and Chili, eating English muffins and talking. But I couldn't. Most of all, I needed to go find Jeremy, tell him about Mercedes, and try to get him to go with me to the fairgrounds.

Chili served her mom's Armenian brunch of shish kebab and stuffed grape leaves, and Tati asked if she could invite Dirk. He arrived looking totally cool with his ponytail and dark jacket. Chili and Paige exchanged expressions of approval with Tati.

Although he admitted, in his proper British accent, that he had never eaten Armenian food, he was soon raving about the *cheese boereg*, which was a combination of puffy pastry, great melted cheese, herbs, and magic. He was also clearly unable to take his eyes from Tati's. *Sorry, Candice and Vanessa. You lose again.*

Once Chili and Paige left for home, I went looking for Jeremy. He wasn't hard to find. The door to his dorm room was open, and guitar music poured out, lovely music, familiar yet fresh and somehow different from anything else I had heard.

I stepped inside, and it stopped.

He put down the guitar and stood. "What Vanessa and Candice did to you sucks."

"I never expected it from Candice," I said. "I wouldn't put anything past Vanessa."

"Don't start on her again."

"It is what it is, Jeremy," I said. "Remember, I saw you together in that room."

"I kissed her, okay? One time. That was all. She was lost, and when I walked into the room, it just kind of happened."

I said. "I saw you together in that room."

"I kissed her, okay? One time. That was all. She was lost, and when I walked into the room, it just kind of happened."

He kissed Vanessa. If I thought about it, I would not be able to do what I must. So I said, "Let's keep our private lives private. I'd like us to work together, and we can't do that if we're fighting about what you did and didn't do all the time."

"Working together hasn't worked very well so far." He smiled at his joke and then moved toward me, slowly, the way the hot guy moves toward the cute girl in every romantic film ever made. "Sit down and tell me what we need to do next."

I didn't sit. I couldn't. "We need to visit the fairgrounds," I said. "Sean Baylor's drummer and his girlfriend said that was where his spirit would be if this *Ghost Seekers* stuff is anything but a hoax."

"Who are you talking about?" We were face-to-face now, so close that I could feel his warm breath. And, yes, I liked it. I knew I shouldn't but still did. "What drummer? What girlfriend?"

"That's what I want to talk to you about," I said. "There's a woman who still writes columns for the newspaper. You missed her the day you showed up, but the security guard connected me with her. She wrote articles about Baylor, but she was also his girlfriend. She's even on the cover of his album. I'm pretty sure that they argued the night he died."

"Are you saying she killed him?"

"I'm not saying anything except that he had a girlfriend, and I talked to her."

"And she admitted it?" he asked. "Admitted that she was his woman?"

"Not yet," I said. "But she will."

"How can you be so sure?"

"She's not the type to lie," I said. "Want to go tomorrow after class?"

"I'd be crazy to." He gave me a look too warm to consider.

His hair had fallen over one eye. It was all I could do to keep from touching it.

"So would I," I said.

"Now that we've settled that . . ." He looked down at his guitar then back up at me. ". . . What time do you want to meet?"

NOTES TO SELF

I have got to forget those soulful eyes of his. Jeremy has crossed me before, and he might be playing games again. I so hope not. Just let him be a true, loyal, Taurus with a faithful Venus in Cancer. Faithful? What am I even thinking?

Later that night, I got a call from my dad. I wasn't sure what it was all about. He was cheerful and upbeat as ever, but there was an uncustomary tightness to his voice. After asking how I was and if I needed anything, he ever so casually said, "By the way, Mom won't be able to be home next weekend."

So that will make three out of three. I started to say it didn't matter but knew he wouldn't be calling me if that were true.

"Let's talk about it when I'm back," I said. "I have a lot going on right now." Was that ever an understatement!

"I'm sorry I called, honey. I just didn't want you to be disappointed."

I told him I was glad that he had called, told him that I loved him. It's pretty clear that I'm not the only one who is disappointed.

25

VENUS ISN'T JUST ABOUT LOVE. IT'S ABOUT HOW YOU
DEAL WITH ALL RELATIONSHIPS. FIND YOUR VENUS,
AND YOU WILL FIND YOUR HEART. AND MAYBE A GREAT
DEAL MORE.

—Fearless Astrology

So my Venus was in wimpy Pisces, the same as my
Moon. That meant as rational as I liked to think I
was, I might just be a secret hopeless romantic.
Thank goodness for my fiery Aries Rising sign. I
already knew that I was spending too much time thinking
about Jeremy and not enough time trying to stay ahead of
him. If tonight worked out, at least we might find out if Sean
Baylor was a ghost or a scam.

Vanessa was subdued in class that Monday. She must have
run out of her constant supply of sweaters, because she had

the red turtleneck on again, zipped to her throat this time. Candice was right beside her with the frozen smile that barely masked the chaos within. Best friends forever—for now, at least. Candice avoided my eyes and remained silent in class.

Jaffa, on the other hand, was upbeat. He praised me, praised Tati, and gave only short answers to Vanessa's few vacuous questions.

Once we were out of the classroom, I forced myself to keep from approaching Jeremy. Paused. I spoke to Tati and Dirk. Waited.

"Hey."

I felt that warm breath on my neck, tried to fight the shiver that spread from there.

"Seven o'clock," he said. "I'll meet you at your room."

He arrived at 6:45.

I opened the door and could only look. The black hair, freshly shampooed—I could smell it—curled around his neck. And he'd put on some kind of scent that made me think of a burning candle. There was a name for it. I just couldn't think of it right then. I couldn't think of much of anything.

"Are you ready?" he asked.

I nodded and closed the door behind me. Let Sean Baylor's ghost show up at the fairgrounds. Let me find some reason for risking my safety and my emotions like this.

Once he pulled onto the deserted fairgrounds, we both sat in Dirk's car and looked out into the starlit darkness. On a raised brick area, a fair poster showed cypress trees silhouetted against an orange sun, much the same as we would soon be.

He turned to me, and I breathed in that scent again. "May seventh," he said. "My birth date."

"I was close." *Right again. Thank you, Fearless.* He really did have Venus in Cancer.

"I don't know how you did it, but I'm going to stop trying to second-guess you, Logan."

Probably not, Mr. Fixed Earth, but it was good to hear.

I started to ask him why he had decided to trust me with his birth date after having accused me of stealing it. Instead, I asked, "So what do you think we ought to do now?"

"I'm trying to decide the best approach," he said. "The place has to have all kinds of security. And there could be some kind of event going on somewhere in there."

"But it's wide open. There must be a way we can get in without anyone seeing us." I reached into my bag. "I printed a map off the Internet."

"You did?"

Ignoring the newfound wonder in his voice, I just did my academic Aquarius bit. "Right here is where I think they must have performed." I tapped a place on the map, the grassy area with three dressing rooms. "It's supposed to hold fifty-eight hundred people, but that weekend in 1967, there were more than two hundred thousand."

"I want to see it." He reached for the car door.

"Not that it matters," I said, "but are you sure it's safe to go out there?"

"No." Those Taurus eyes met mine, and I fought the urge to turn away.

Instead, I returned the look. "All right then. Let's get started."

We got out of the car, and he slung his guitar over his shoulder. Then we moved around the exterior of the stark fairgrounds until we found the opening I had located on the map.

"Do you think playing Baylor's songs will summon his spirit?" I asked.

"Maybe, but not the way you mean. I just want to know how it felt."

"What do you mean?"

"Those musicians, all those years ago before we were born. And Sean Baylor. He wasn't much older than I am now."

I knew he had probably done the same research that I had, but it seemed more personal to him, maybe because he was a musician.

"It's considered one of the beginnings of the Summer of Love." The minute I said, the L-word, I felt myself flush.

He reached out, took my hand, and squeezed.

"It's quite a place. You can feel it, can't you?"

"I can," I said, and it wasn't a lie.

Once inside, it was if there were ghosts descending like thick, teasing fog with every step I took. The misty air was like slender icicles that slid beneath my scarf and along my neck.

I pulled the scarf tighter. He let go of me and shoved his

hands into the pockets of his jacket.

"Okay, I admit it," I said. "This place scares the hell out of me."

"Me, too." He put his arm around me. "Maybe this isn't such a good idea, Logan. I know that Baylor isn't out here, but maybe something else is. I don't want you to get hurt."

"We have our phones," I said. "If it gets weird, I can call Tati. Or you could call Dirk."

"No way." It was that sharp laugh, one of the few things I disliked about him, because it sounded meaner than he was. "He's only interested in the women. I don't have anyone here I can count on, only . . ." His voice trailed off, but I saw the rest of it in his expression.

Only you. That's what he was going to say.

"I know you need to do this," I told him, "and maybe I do too. That place over there looks about right. See the grass and the stage wrapped around it?" I didn't have to mention that it was deserted and scary beyond belief. I was sure he already knew that.

"You're right." He ran the rest of the way up to it, and when he turned back to me, his face reflected in the moonlight. He seemed to be transformed. His hair appeared longer, wild in the cold breeze. And his eyes were so large, so shadowed, that if I didn't know better, I would be afraid.

He looked like one of the black-and-white posters I had found online. I could see the music and the memories in his eyes. A thought floated through my mind. *What if Baylor's ghost really does exist? What if I'm looking at him?*

"Come up there with me." He took my hand and helped me up onto the stage. Then he settled beside me on the edge of it and plucked the guitar strings with his finger.

I knew the melody by now.

"No," I said.

He ignored me and began to sing.

"Was all we had to say to each other all we had to say to each other? Was forever only a feeling we shared for just one night?"

He sounded like Sean Baylor. And, yes, he looked like him—those pale eyes, darker at the edges of the pupils. The shaggy, black hair catching the breeze as if alive. I realized that I was trembling.

"You were right. I really should leave now."

He didn't seem to hear. Instead, he changed the song, a frenetic guitar solo that chilled me as much as the fog had.

"I said I have to go now," I told him. "There aren't any ghosts out here, and if there are, they probably don't want to be disturbed."

"What's wrong?" He stopped playing and reached for me.

I pulled away. "This is creepy."

"It's wonderful. Don't you get it, Logan? He might have sat right here."

"I understand that, but I still want to go back," I said. "I have a lot of things going on in my life right now."

"Like what?"

"My mom and dad." I couldn't believe I was saying this to

him. "They fight all of the time because she's always on a golf tour and never home."

"Big deal. Your folks are having problems. At least they're around you."

"My mom isn't," I said. "She's gone most of the year. She didn't even come back the way she said she would when I went home for the weekend."

"At least you know where she is. At least she knows you exist."

"What are you trying to say?" I reached for his hand and held on tightly.

"My father," he said. "He doesn't know I'm alive. If I don't find him, he never will know."

"Where do you think he is?" I asked.

"That's what I came to Monterey to find out. The real reason. And I am living proof that he's no ghost."

Then it started to make sense, just a little. The way he looked. His voice. Still clutching his hand, I tried to find the right words.

"Are you trying to tell me what I think you are?"

He looked into my eyes. "I'm trying to tell you that Sean Baylor is my father."

I shivered. "That's impossible." But it wasn't. In fact, now it all made sense. Why a musician would try to win a writing contest. Why Jeremy had wanted to come to Monterey. "You're hoping that someone who knows him will see your article and tell him that he has a son."

"Right."

"That's one way," I said. "I have some other ideas too."

"I'd like to hear them." He gave me this odd smile that turned into a hug, and then, a kiss. And, yes, I was kissing Jeremy Novack in the creepiest night-time venue in Monterey. And, yes, I'd never felt this sure about anything until this moment of my life.

"I don't know what to do with you," he whispered.

I ran my fingers into his wonderful hair and drew his face next to mine.

"Maybe we should try to figure it out. Together."

I could vaguely hear the sounds of cars hurrying past, maybe even the ocean, and whatever ghosts the fog hid. Then he kissed me again, and I knew I would do whatever I must to help him, even if the cost was my own heart.

NOTES TO SELF

We talked. Over coffee, over burgers, and finally, overlooking the ocean. According to Jeremy, Sean Baylor had been performing under another name when he met Jeremy's mom at a club in New York in the early nineties. They spent a couple of weeks together before he moved on, unaware that she had figured out his true identity. I understand now why Jeremy wants his article to be selected for the anthology. He is hoping Sean or someone who knows him will see it. I only hope Mercedes can help me fill in some blanks about what happened that night. And, if Baylor really is Jeremy's father, he could not have died in 1967. Maybe Jeremy still has a chance to find him.

I can't sleep tonight and probably won't. I just kissed Jeremy. I just kissed Sean Baylor's son. And if that is true, if Baylor isn't haunting the restaurant, who is?

26

Trust is a precious commodity. The Fire signs (Aries, Leo, and Sagittarius) want to be trusted but don't always work to earn it. The Air signs (Gemini, Libra, and Aquarius) talk about trust. The Earth signs (Taurus, Virgo, and Capricorn) take it to heart and frequently come through. The Water signs (Cancer, Scorpio, and Pisces), emotionally connected to issues and people, can seldom risk it and know from experience that they could suffer betrayal if they do. Whatever your sign, value trust. Life would work better if we all trusted more.

—Fearless Astrology

nable to sleep, I figured out the rest of Jeremy's chart early Tuesday morning. A Taurus with his Mars in emotional Cancer. Okay, I had to admit, Jeremy and I were both Fixed signs, both opinionated. While Taurus charges, Aquarius pulls away. Still, both share a strong desire to succeed. Maybe that would keep us connected. Maybe what we shared last night would be as real as it had felt at the time.

I walked into class with Tati and Dirk. For once, Jeremy was there ahead of us, in the same dark clothes, the same dark hair, the same dark expression. He glanced up at me, and his eyes lit up like a lamp in a pitch-black room. His lips reminded me all too well of last night.

I went straight to him.

"Hey, Logan," Vanessa said. "In case you don't remember, this is my seat."

"Keep it." Jeremy shrugged and then walked with me to the front.

"Whatever," she called from behind us. "Losers."

"Vanessa." We all jerked our heads toward Jaffa.

"What, Henry?"

"See me after class."

"Not again. I only meant . . ."

"After class," he repeated. If he had used that voice on me, I would have had to leave the workshop and jump into the ocean.

Vanessa knew no shame. She fluffed her hair, crossed her

legs, and grinned up at Jaffa. "I didn't think it proper to mention this before, Henry, but a guy in here has been hitting on me. How can I go about reporting him?"

I sensed Jeremy squirm. Oh, great. We were now going to have the great confession about the kiss at the restaurant, which would be followed by Jaffa banishing Jeremy from the workshop.

"Vanessa," Jaffa said, in a weary voice. "I have already told you that we can speak after class. Would you please respect my wishes?" To the rest of us, he said, "Rik McNeil and the *Ghost Seekers* crew will be here on Wednesday. It will be a rare opportunity for all of you, regardless of your topics. And speaking of your topics, I'd like you all to read from your work today."

Vanessa whispered to Candice, who asked, "What part of our work?" *So now it was the Vanessa and Candice Show.* It was stupid of her to speak up so fast after Vanessa had obviously directed her to.

"That is your choice." Jaffa tossed off his scarf as if the room had grown too warm for him. "Logan, could you clarify?"

Everyone turned to look at me. I glanced over at Jeremy. He was wearing his usual arrogant mask, but when our eyes met, he gave me a smile so brief that I almost missed it.

I smiled back and turned to Jaffa. "You've already looked at our leads," I said, "and you told us the lead should be followed by the first major point the writer wants to make. That's what I brought."

"Would you read it for us?" Jaffa asked.

Vanessa sighed so loudly that I almost expected him to kick her out on the spot.

I looked down at my paper. "Ghost or no ghost, with his Gemini Sun, Sean Baylor would never depart without keeping an eye on the past. The Air sign of Gemini is far too curious."

"Excellent, Logan." Jaffa was clearly starting to like me. "Again, you've created questions, and questions create reader interest."

After we left class, Jeremy and I walked back to the dorms. He held my hand, and I was more determined than ever to help him find out what had happened to Sean Baylor.

"Where do we go next?" he asked. The *we* sounded right and natural, but not for what I had to do now.

"I'm going to find Mercedes and try to get her to tell me what happened the night Sean—I mean, your father—disappeared."

"I thought we were working together." How quickly the distrust transformed his expression and his voice. As if he lived on the brink of doubt.

"We *are* working together," I said. "But, in case you haven't noticed, you look just like your father."

"Ren Baylor hasn't picked up on that."

"That's because she isn't aware of anyone but herself."

"I always wondered why he would want to disappear. I'm sure having her for a sister was part of it."

"Lucky that she didn't notice the resemblance," I told him.

"Mercedes, though. She's used to digging for information. We don't know why your father disappeared, but it's pretty clear that he doesn't want it made public."

He pulled me to him and lifted my chin so that our eyes met. "Is that the only reason you don't want me to go with you? Because you think Mercedes might figure it out?"

I jerked away. "What's it going to take for me to prove myself to you?"

"You *have* proven yourself. I just don't have much experience trusting anyone. Other than my mom, of course."

"Mars in Cancer," I said. "It makes sense. But you're going to have to trust me if we're going to find out what happened to your father."

"Please don't get all crazy on me with the astro stuff."

"Astrology is not crazy," I said. "Cancers frequently have mother issues, and even more of them have family issues. I need to go now, Jeremy. I don't want to miss Mercedes."

"Please." He reached out, took my hand, and squeezed it. "I don't want you going there alone."

"Why not? She seems okay."

"Except that she was the last one seen with my father. You say they fought. What if she tried to kill him? You could be in danger."

Now, that was something I hadn't considered. "You think so?"

"Let me drive you, at least," he said. "I'll wait in the car if you think that's the best way. Just don't go there by yourself."

I felt my willpower dissolving like sand under the tide. He had that kind of dangerous pull on me.

"All right," I said. "If you promise to stay far enough away. If she sees you, I know she'll figure it out."

"You asked what it would take." He turned and slid his arms around my waist. I wanted to just stand like this and relish the warmth. "The answer is that you don't have to prove anything to me, Logan. I really think I trust you."

In spite of his adoring expression, I felt a little let down. "*Think* is cool," I said. "Let me know when you truly trust me. I can find Mercedes on my own."

"Logan, wait."

No time. I couldn't risk having Mercedes figure out who he was.

If he was. Now, I was the one doing the doubting, and I didn't like the way it felt.

NOTES TO SELF

Must be my fiery Aries Rising, because it certainly wasn't my pondering Aquarius Sun. I simply walked away from him. Still, I'm hoping that there will be a time when we will speak about it. When maybe he can explain why he can't trust me completely. But that conversation won't be happening today.

27

THE HIGHEST POINT THE SUN REACHES DURING THE DAY IS CALLED MID-HEAVEN OR TENTH HOUSE. THE PLANET IN THIS HOUSE REFLECTS YOUR GOALS, CAREERS, AUTHORITY FIGURES, AND THE INFLUENCE OF YOUR MOTHER OVER YOUR CHOICES IN LIFE. STUDY THIS PLACEMENT IN ORDER TO UNDERSTAND AND OVERCOME CAREER ROADBLOCKS AND ALSO TO BUILD UPON STRENGTHS THAT YOU ALREADY HAVE.

—Fearless Astrology

corpio was in my Tenth House. Emotional, fixed, often stuck in the past, not a quitter. Also secretive and loyal. And as for my mother, that was a little freaky. Maybe what was going on with Dad and her was getting to me more than I pretended. And, yes, I was emotional about wanting to get ahead. Today, I was going to use that Tenth House tenacity to get what I needed from Mercedes.

I took a taxi to the newspaper office. Richard, my go-to security guard, wasn't around. The guard on duty was about twenty, my height, and female.

"I'm here to see Mercedes," I said.

"Down the hall in the break room." The guard pointed and then looked down at her magazine. She wasn't nearly as friendly as Richard. I hoped that she wasn't his replacement, and that maybe this was only his day off.

She returned to her reading, and I walked in the direction she had indicated. The hall gleamed, and I realized that the ugly green carpet had been replaced. The elevator door had been painted black, or maybe I was turned around. It wasn't an elevator at all, only a recessed area in the middle of the hall.

Ahead, I saw a room full of vending machines reflected by the surreal brightness of florescent light. The only window faced the hall where I stood. Mercedes sat at a round white picnic table. She wore a long gray skirt and a black sweater that contrasted with her frizzy silver hair.

I stared at her through the window for a moment. Her head was bent forward, and she was massaging her neck with one hand. Tired, I thought, or maybe just thinking the way my dad did sometimes when he didn't know I was looking.

She looked up. I gave a little wave and stepped through the swinging door.

"Observing me, were you?" she said.

"I just wanted to be sure I was in the right room." It was all I could do to hide my embarrassment and try not to sound defensive. "You mentioned that you don't use your old office."

"I couldn't if I wanted to." She seemed to consider whether or not to let me off the hook for spying on her. "I e-mail most of my columns, but today I delivered the disc and spent time with some of my old friends."

I stood across from her at the table, still afraid to sit. "Thank you for agreeing to talk to me again."

"I'm having second thoughts about that."

"Why?" I gripped the back of the chair.

"Ren Baylor. She came to see me. We had a long talk."

"So, you're friends now?" I asked.

"Hardly. But the fastest way to reconcile past differences is to find a common enemy. Remember that if you pursue investigative reporting."

"What common enemy?" She gave me a penetrating look. "Are you talking about me?"

She nodded. "Ren feels you are—and these are her words— immature and meddling. I still have some contacts at the college. Not as powerful as hers. She wants us to join together to use those contacts."

"To help her get me thrown out?" I felt miserable. Scared.

"Or at least to shut up."

"You can't do that," I said. "Please don't."

She pulled out the chair beside her. "Sit down, will you?

Frankly it's not my style to pull strings, but, for once in her life, Ren has a point."

"Which is?"

"That, astrology or not, you are very young, Logan. Too young to be trying to investigate what happened to Sean Baylor, even with Henry Jaffa's blessings. You can't possibly understand."

"You were young when you fell in love with Sean Baylor. How would you feel if someone had told you that you couldn't possibly understand?"

Her cheeks flushed a deep pink, and I'm sure mine were doing the same.

"Where did you hear that?"

"From Cookie."

"Cookie Burke? How do you know him?"

"I've talked to him twice. He's not hard to find, as I'm sure you know."

"I haven't looked for him, and you shouldn't have either."

"You can't mean that. You're a reporter."

"And an adult," she said. "I think it's irresponsible of Jaffa to allow this."

"Because I'm young?" I asked.

"Because you're inexperienced."

"So were you once. Someone had to give you a chance. Remember how you felt when you were my age? What if someone had told you that you were too young to be with Sean?"

"*I* was in love," she said, "and I'm not ashamed of it."

I thought of Jeremy's lips and the smell of his hair when it brushed against my face in the cold wind.

"Cookie said you and Sean argued that night."

"On the boat." She leaned across the table. "Yes, that's how I spent my last moments with him. On that boat, screaming at each other. Write that if you want. Now, please leave."

So, I had been right. I willed my voice to remain steady. "What were you arguing about?"

"The future. Ren thinks I had something to do with his death. That's ridiculous, of course."

I tried again. "Why were you fighting?"

She pushed back her chair. "You're the journalism student. You tell me."

I tried to think about why these two Air signs, Gemini and Libra, could be so angry with each other. "He was a Gemini, and maybe there were some infidelity issues there. Maybe there were conflicts about goals. Maybe you wanted to move him faster into the limelight than he did. And maybe his Water sign sister wanted more control than he could tolerate."

"You're good." She fiddled with her hair, and I could tell she was nervous. "How much of that did you learn through astrology, and how much by investigative reporting?"

"I don't know." I said. "Maybe fifty-fifty."

"Are you really convinced that Sean's ghost is haunting Monterey?"

"I know, for a fact, that it's not."

"What could make you so sure?"

"I mean," I said quickly, "I know there are spirits, or whatever you want to call them, at the restaurant and probably other places in town. I just don't think Sean Baylor is one of them. Cookie doesn't think so either. I guess we'll find out when *Ghost Seekers* shows up tomorrow."

"Sean would hate that so much," she said. "It was all about the music for him. That's why we fought. Between his sister and me, the poor guy didn't stand a chance."

"What was he going to do?" I asked. "Stop performing?"

She shook her head, and her smile was so sad that it hurt me to look into her eyes. "He wanted to walk away from everything that happened at the festival that night—all of that attention, the fame—and he wanted me to go to Ireland with him. Change our names and go to freaking Ireland so that he could sing in a pub."

"And that was a bad thing?"

Her expression went hard, and I knew she was fighting tears. "At the time, I thought so. Today, I wish I had gone. Even if we hadn't made it as a couple, we would have tried, and he would not be dead. Sometimes, trying is good enough, you know?"

"I know." It was all I could do to hide my own tears.

"You wanted a story. There's the story," she said. "Don't say I didn't give you a chance. I hope your dream works out better than mine did."

We walked out together. The security guard looked up from her magazine only briefly.

"What happened to Richard?" I asked Mercedes.

"Richard?"

"The other security guard. Short, stocky. Wears a lot of scent. He seemed to know you."

"Now, what are you trying to pull?" She squared off from me on the street, no longer vulnerable. It was my first glimpse of this cynical side of her, and I didn't know what to do.

"Nothing," I said. "I talked to him the first time I came here. When he found me upstairs, he showed me where your office is."

"*Where my office was.* The second floor has been sealed off for years."

"That can't be right," I said. "I was up there."

"And now I'm supposed to say that the top floor has been closed since the fire." She crossed her arms. "Then you're supposed to say *what fire*. And finally, you'll go off and write whatever ghostly *something* you need to impress Henry Jaffa, right?"

"Wrong," I said, "but I know what I saw, and I saw a second floor with people working on it. I saw a security guard named Richard."

"That is impossible."

"Believe me or don't. It's the truth, and I don't have any reason to lie to you."

"Except that a security guard named Richard was trapped in the elevator when the fire broke out that night back in the eighties. There was a lot about it in the news then. It should not be too difficult for a young, ambitious reporter to find."

"I didn't," I said. "Obviously, the guard I spoke with was someone else. Thanks for you your time." I walked away from her in a daze.

NOTES TO SELF

That would be something—if I had channeled the security guard, or just as scary, had imagined him. But I couldn't have. Richard was as real as I was. Wasn't he? Even though Mercedes doubted me, she had given me a chance by telling me the truth about her conflict with Baylor. So all he wanted to do was escape and sing in a pub someplace? But he was a curious Gemini, who would have had to know what was going on. Someone who would have to have a secretive Scorpio pal, for instance. I think about Jeremy, his arms around me, and try to tell myself to let it end here. Let Jeremy write his paper and hope for the best. Encourage him to move to Monterey, and not do the one thing I must do. The one thing that, if I am successful, will surely take him from me.

28

WE ALL HAVE A PAST. WE ALL HAVE A FUTURE. BUT ALL
WE REALLY HAVE IS RIGHT NOW. YOU CAN CHANGE YOUR
DESTINY IN ONE MOMENT, IF ONLY YOU REFUSE TO DO
WHAT YOU ONCE DID. THIS IS EASIER FOR SOME SIGNS
THAN IT IS FOR OTHERS. IF YOU ARE A FIXED TAURUS,
LEO, SCORPIO, OR AQUARIUS, FIGHT YOUR NATURAL
INCLINATION TO DO WHAT YOU HAVE ALWAYS DONE OR
WHAT YOU FEEL SAFE DOING. TAKE A CHANCE.

—*Fearless Astrology*

would need to remember that advice from *Fearless
Astrology* tonight—to act instead of ponder.

Ghost Seekers arrived, and it appeared that everyone in the workshop wanted to be part of the show, except
Jaffa. He seemed almost pained and told us repeatedly that

he might be changing our *venue* if *certain people* tried to influence his workshop. I knew that he meant Ren Baylor and her trying to get me booted from the college.

That Wednesday night, we all gathered at the restaurant again. It was different this time. A film crew crowded the entrance. A cute guy wearing an olive-green shirt walked around the room greeting people as if it were his party. It was.

Aries Rik McNeil. How many times had I watched that sculpted face on television? A radio personality in Las Vegas before his success with *Ghost Seekers*, his easy-going manner and apparent lack of ego had made him stand out from other reality show hosts. His knowledge of what he called, "the other side" had done the rest. Now, he was walking up to me as if we were old friends.

"You're one of the kids who heard the music, right?" he asked and put out his hand. "I'm Rik." *As if I didn't know.*

"Logan," I said.

We shook, and he said, "Doug and Emily told me that you heard Sean Baylor singing upstairs."

"I heard a song. I'm not sure who the singer was, though."

"Great. If you don't mind, would you join those other two girls by the staircase?" His voice was both mellow and raspy. I could imagine it on a car radio late at night.

"I don't think I should be on the show," I told him. "I don't believe Baylor's ghost was anywhere around here."

"A nonbeliever, huh?" He couldn't quite keep the question from sounding condescending.

"That's not what I'm trying to say," I told him. "I know there are spirits here. I just don't think Sean Baylor's is."

"Why's that?"

Because I don't think he's dead.

"I don't know. Just not here."

"Okay." He nodded pleasantly enough, and I knew that I had not convinced him. "Those two girls over there really do want to be on the show. Join them, and we can work out the details as we go along."

I headed where he had directed me. Then I looked over and saw Candice and Vanessa in their skinny little jeans and matching black jackets. They could be twins, except that Vanessa hair's was dark and Candice's was light. And Vanessa's jacket was unzipped as low as she dared, and Candice's was most definitely not.

He seemed to sense my hesitation. "Is there a problem?" he asked. "Are you concerned that your intuitive powers will be weaker around them?"

It sounded good enough to me. "Kind of like that."

"You know what we're doing here? If it really is Sean Baylor's spirit—or anyone's—our job is just to help it move on."

I wanted to tell him that it was not Sean Baylor's spirit. Instead, I asked, "How does a spirit move on?"

"Maybe because, for some reason, it's stuck here, on our plane. Violent death. Suicide. Unfinished business." Although he seemed to be focused only on me, I could tell he was also checking out how many people were filling the room.

"Why can only certain people see them?" I asked, and thought about Richard, the security guard.

"Why question? Perhaps we're selected for a reason." He lowered his voice again. "Okay, why don't you hang out on the other side of the room with the girl who lost consciousness?"

"That works." I walked happily toward Tati.

"Thanks," she said. "Fainting disqualifies me, I guess. Those girls are the A team for interviews."

"Let them go for it, then. We don't have to be interviewed to write about what happens."

Just then, Jeremy walked in, and without acknowledging the cameras or the host, headed toward us. The moment our eyes met, I knew that we would get through this night together. This night, and maybe a great many more.

"Hey, Tati." He patted her arm. "How are you doing?"

"Apparently *persona non grata* tonight," she said. "Because I fainted, I'm not a reliable source for *Ghost Seekers.*"

"And those two girls are?" I asked.

Candice and Vanessa flashed us nasty looks, as if they could hear what we were saying.

"You have a problem?" Tati asked.

"Bitch," Vanessa shot back.

"Cool it, will you, guys?" Rik said. "Forget the camera. Forget me. Think instead about the spirits trapped here on this plane. Think about how you wish to learn all you can to help free them."

It was difficult to forget him, since he was standing right

next to me, but I tried. Not for Baylor's sake, of course, but for the spirits that really were trapped here.

And then, the music began. Soft at first, just enough to raise the hairs along my neck. Then, louder. I wasn't imagining this. Someone, something was trying to be heard. I reached for Jeremy's hand and felt him reaching for mine. Our fingers connected and clasped. I held on tightly.

> *Was all we had to say to each other*
> *All we had to say to each other?*
> *Was forever only a feeling . . .*

It was happening again. I gasped in spite of myself. Jeremy pulled me closer.

The room seemed to freeze with fear. Beside me, Rik grew still, like a cat waiting to pounce.

On the upper level, a man appeared. Not a man, a shadow of one. He had long dark hair and a guitar draped around him. Sean Baylor. No, not Sean Baylor. It couldn't be.

"I'm going up there," I whispered. "You take the stairs."

I slipped away from the group and sneaked into the elevator. I hit the button for the second floor, where I had first heard Baylor's music.

It opened with a sigh. I stepped out and ran into the man who was trying to get on, the guitar still slung around his neck.

"What the hell?" He grabbed me and tried to shove me back inside. Even in the disguise, I recognized him. The gold stud he hadn't bothered to remove from his ear. The stench of smoke.

"Jeremy," I screamed. "Help me. It's the boat guy."

"Shut up." He shoved me, and I hit the floor hard. My vision was blurred, but I could still see his eyes, still see his black boots coming closer.

I tried to squirm away from him and looked down over the balcony at the horrified faces, then back up at him. To my shock, he looked panicked.

"He's trying to push her over the edge," I heard Rik shout. "Let's get up there."

"They're coming," I said, stunned at how slurred and slow my words came out.

He turned and ran into the shadows.

Jeremy was the first one to reach me, then Jaffa, then Rik McNeil. The three of them helped me to my feet. Tati joined us, and I realized that she had been crying.

"Do you know how close you came?" she asked. "Who would do this?"

I thought about Ren Baylor and wondered if she were crazy enough to want to see me dead. That didn't make any sense. If Ren wanted to hire someone to kill me, she had enough money to make it happen. Besides, the guy with the gold stud was an amateur. He came after me only because I had discovered him.

We all went downstairs together. Rik and his crew were busy on their cell phones. Vanessa moved to the corner behind the stairs, leaned down, and picked up something. Dark hair curtained her face. What I could see of her expression was rare concentration. She had picked up a phone, and now, she was frantically tapping the keypad.

"Wait a minute," I told Jeremy.

"What?"

"Look at Vanessa. She's not calling anyone. Something else is going on."

She must have heard me because she turned and gave me an evil look. "Do you have a problem, Logan?"

I moved toward her and yanked the phone out of her hands.

"Give it back."

I pressed every button I could find. I finally found her downloaded music. I pressed again, and Baylor's voice flooded the room.

Was all we had to say to each other . . .

"You," I whispered.

Jaffa rushed to my side. "Vanessa," he said, then shook his head as if clueless as to how he should continue.

"She faked it," I said. "Sean Baylor's spirit was never here. Vanessa got some help." Then I thought about all of the time she spent at the theater downtown. "I'll bet he's an actor."

"No big." Vanessa grinned at Jaffa. "As you know, Henry, all I wanted from this workshop was a role in your new TV movie. My dad said to improvise and use my best talents.

You've got to admit I did a pretty amazing job."

"Amazing?" he asked in that icy tone. "Acting is not faking. Logan could have been killed." He turned to the rest of us. "You kids stay here."

"I'm going with you," Jeremy said.

"Me, too." My head throbbed, but I didn't care.

NOTES TO SELF

Jeremy and Jaffa found the guy hiding on the balcony. He admitted that he and Vanessa had met at the theater, and that she had hired him to pretend to be Sean Baylor in the restaurant, and later, at the beach. It was a chance at some great publicity, he said. He hadn't meant to hurt me. About that time, the two police officers came through the door.

All Vanessa had wanted from the beginning was a role in Jaffa's TV movie. She might have gotten it if she had managed to fool Rik McNeil and *Ghost Seekers*. It's been an ecstatic celebration for those of us who chose to hang around tonight. The TV people are treating us like stars. We have won.

And I have lost. I have lost for reasons I don't even want to think about right now.

29

LOVE IS COMPLEX, AND IT IS POSSIBLE FOR ANY TWO
SIGNS TO BUILD A LOVING RELATIONSHIP. THE STUDY
OF ASTROLOGY IS NOT TO LIMIT YOUR OPPORTUNITIES
BUT TO EXPAND THEM. STUDY THE COMPATIBILITY OF
YOUR SIGNS. KNOW WHERE YOUR DIFFERENCES AND
CHALLENGES LIE. IF YOU REALLY CARE, FOLLOW, NOT
THE ZODIAC, BUT YOUR OWN HEART.

—*Fearless Astrology*

nited/Untied. Switch two letters and change your
destiny. This is probably not the best time for me
to be reading the love-match section of *Fearless*
Thursday morning, but I couldn't help it.

Aquarius: eccentric and seeker of security.
Taurus: sensual and committed. It might have worked.

Jaffa announced that today would be our last class. Instead, he will finish Friday with one-on-one meetings with us. Last night, he told me how sorry he was that he allowed me to be put in danger, and he apologized for what he called "Vanessa's unconscionable behavior." She was no longer part of the workshop.

I know he likes me, but I also know that there isn't a chance that my article will win. It can't begin to compete with Jeremy's.

Someone knocked on my door early Thursday morning. On the bunk across from me, Tati snoozed on.

Jeremy? If only.

I slipped out of bed and opened the door. Candice stood there, looking like the victim she must believe she was.

"It's a little late for apologies," I said.

She shook her head. "I just wanted to say goodbye. I'm leaving, but, yes, I am sorry, Logan."

"What about Vanessa?"

"She's leaving too. So you win again. Just the way my sisters always do."

"If you'd change your approach, maybe you might change the outcome."

"Right." She shook her head as if totally disgusted with me. "If you had sibs like mine, maybe you wouldn't be so smug."

"And if you had no sibs, maybe you wouldn't have been so ready to hate me."

"I don't hate you. I never did. Actually . . ." Her voice

trailed off. "I did show Vanessa your book, but I had no idea she'd hooked up with that actor and gotten him to pretend to be Baylor. I'm sorry, okay?" Then she shrugged and walked away.

So now, I had only two tasks remaining in this workshop. Finish my article, which would not win. And be the altruistic Aquarius that I was, and go see Cookie Burke.

Vanessa and Candice were not in class. Henry Jaffa didn't mention why, but everyone seemed to know. Jeremy and I sat together. He shot me sad looks throughout the lecture. I did my best. But what could I say about Sean Baylor compared to what he would? I had the singer's astro vibe nailed. But Jeremy was his son. He had told Jaffa that at the beginning of class. Although Jaffa had allowed him to write his own Baylor piece, he had not believed Jeremy. Soon he would. Once he knew the truth.

That night, Dirk and Tati were working together in our room on the last parts of their articles. Jeremy borrowed Dirk's car, and I directed him to the club where Cookie played.

"Why are we going here?" Jeremy squeezed my hand. "All I want is to be alone with you."

"You trust me, don't you?"

He nodded. "Finally. Yes, I do."

"Then trust me enough to wait out here until I find out what I need to."

"If you're not out in ten minutes, you know I'll be all over the place."

"Ten minutes?" I looked back into those eyes and wanted to cry. "Sure. I can probably do that."

Bernie, the cocktail server, had a cell phone pressed to her ear. Her hair was pulled up in back, and I could see the beginnings of perpendicular lines intersecting her lips.

She saw me and spoke into her phone. "I'll call you when I get off. I have a customer."

"I'm here to see Cookie," I told her.

"Only if it's okay with him."

"It is."

Cookie was sitting in the same booth, with what looked like the same drink. Only his shirt had changed. Today it was a deep ruby color that matched the stone of his ring. I sat down without waiting for an invitation. He glanced up at me with eyes entrenched in sorrow.

"Hey, kid. I got nothing else to say."

"I do." I said. "I found out what happened with Mercedes and Sean Baylor."

"You get around." He smiled with his lips. His eyes revealed nothing. "I guess the whole haunting thing at the restaurant was some kind of fake. I caught something about it on the news."

"Part of it," I said. "As you know, Sean Baylor couldn't be haunting the restaurant or anywhere else in Monterey, because he isn't dead."

"That's it." He slammed his hand on the table. "Bernie, get this kid out of here."

"Wait a minute," I said. "I know Baylor's alive, and I know you're the only one he can trust. If you let that woman throw me out of here, you won't stop me. I will find him, sooner or later, if I have to go all the way to Ireland."

His sad expression changed to one of fear.

"Okay, honey." The woman approached our table, all business in her sequined tuxedo shirt. "I need to see your ID, or you have to go."

"I'll leave in a moment," I said. "I need to talk to Cookie about a mutual friend."

"Cookie?" She caught his eye.

"Give me a minute," he said.

"Make up your mind, will you?" She stalked off, clearly disgusted.

"What do you want?" Cookie asked. "Are you doing some kind of crazy blackmail scheme? Because if you are . . ."

"All I want is for you to come with me to the parking lot. Sean Baylor's son is out there."

"Now you've pushed me too far." But he didn't move.

"Baylor had a son," I said. "His name is Jeremy, and he looks just like his father. He has a photo of his mother and Baylor."

"Sean B. would never desert his own kid," he said flatly.

"He doesn't know about him." I got up from the table. "Finding his father is the most important thing in Jeremy's life. Please, come with me."

We walked together to the car. In spite of the cold, Jeremy

stood outside, chin lifted, with arms crossed in front of his jacket, tangled hair blowing across his face. *Thinking what? I wondered. How could I hope to be in that equation?*

Beside me, Cookie stopped.

Jeremy nodded to me, then looked at him, and without musical accompaniment, began to sing.

Was all we had to say to each other . . .

Cookie's eyes grew wide. "You look just like him," he said.

"I should. He's my father. I'll take any test he wants."

Cookie shook his head slowly. "He didn't know. He *doesn't* know. I swear."

"Where is he? Will you take me to him?"

"Far away from here, but he'll want to see you. I can tell you that." Cookie's entire personality changed. His raw voice became intimate and friendly. "You've got to be about the same age as my youngest boy. How come you're only now coming forward?"

"Because I knew that he must have disappeared for a reason," Jeremy said. "If it hadn't been for Logan . . ." They both turned to look at me.

"You were the key," I told Cookie. "You take it from here."

I no longer belonged with them. They needed to talk alone, and it was still early enough for me to be able to find a cab.

"You're not going anywhere." Jeremy pulled me to him. "Let's go inside and figure out what to do."

We went back into the club. Cookie got on the telephone. Jeremy and I held hands and waited.

"Sean B.?" Cookie lowered his voice. "Man, you aren't going to believe what I have to tell you."

Jeremy took Cookie's phone and walked to the other side of the club.

"I know Sean, and he's going to want some changes," Cookie told me. "Everything Ren Baylor has, it should be the boy's."

"Do you think she suspected that Sean was alive?" I asked.

"No telling." He looked down at his hands, the deep ruby stone on his finger. "She sure had to be keeping tabs on me, though, to know right away that you'd come in that night."

"I know," I said. "Remember how dead it was in here? There wasn't anyone around except . . ."

I realized that the blond server was standing beside the booth, stone-faced. The sequins on her black tuxedo shirt glittered in the dim lights. Her eyes looked dead.

"You're the one who told Ren Baylor," I said.

Cookie looked at her carefully as if trying to read her expression, except there was nothing to read. She was a blank slate. "Don't just stand there, Bernie. Tell the kid she's nuts."

"You know I think the world of you." She shrugged in that weary way of hers. "What can I say? I needed the money."

"Ren Baylor paid you to keep tabs on me? You agreed to that?"

"Just since all of this ghost stuff started. You understand, don't you, Cookie? It wasn't personal. You'd do the same thing if the shoe was on the other foot."

"No I wouldn't. I didn't, not in all these years."

He got up from the table, and she stepped back as if afraid he would strike her. "When you check in with that no-good woman, be sure to tell her that Sean B. is alive," he said. "Tell her he spoke to his son tonight."

NOTES TO SELF

Later, Jeremy and I ended up on the wharf, holding hands, kissing, and finally, getting something to eat from one of the seafood stands.

"I'll never smell fish and chips without thinking about you and this night," he told me.

I wonder if he is right. Years from now, will I smell the ocean and the scent of frying food and remember him?

This has easily been the most wonderful night of my life—and the saddest. Because I know that Jeremy cares about me, and because I also know what he must do next.

30

TAURUS CAN BE ABRUPT, EVEN CRUEL. BUT THAT IS NOT THE WAY THE BULL SEES IT. THE BULL SEES IT AS THE TRUTH ACCORDING TO TAURUS. IF YOU FALL IN LOVE WITH A BULL, YOU MUST UNDERSTAND THAT TAURUS ANGER DOES NOT CANCEL TAURUS TRUTH— NOR DOES IT CANCEL TAURUS LOVE.

—Fearless Astrology

know that now. I have seen Jeremy abrupt, and I have seen him angry. But I have also seen the goodness in him, his capacity for deep feelings. His face last night, when he first spoke to his father on Cookie's phone, is something I will never forget. It made me know that I did the right thing by insisting that we go to the club.

Cookie admitted that Sean faked his disappearance to escape the life his controlling sister had mapped out for him.

He never wanted to be a star, and he hated the kind of person he was becoming. He is at peace in Ireland, and now that he knows about Sean, he no longer wants to hide. I wonder what Ren Baylor will do when Bernie gives her the good news. I wonder if Sean and Mercedes will get back together, or if Sean and Jeremy will just stay in Ireland and forget about those of us in their pasts.

Even though Jeremy promises to return, I know that the summer and the boy I care for will soon be gone. I get up early and dress in the darkness to keep from waking Tati. Paige loaned me her Pucci top because, she said, the wild swirls of blue and green set off my eyes.

Before I meet him this morning, I take a walk on the beach, over the ice plant, all of those choked roots that refuse to let go. Down to the water, where Jeremy and I first tried to outsmart each other but accidentally fell for each other instead. Maybe that's wrong. Perhaps I fell for him the moment he grabbed my hand when Vanessa shoved me into his lap on the ghost trolley that night.

On the way back, I run into Jaffa. He's wearing a pair of baggy beige shorts and a jacket.

"Getting used to our weather, are you?" I ask.

"I'd better be. I'm going to live here at least another six months. Sean Baylor's ghost was faked, but there are plenty of other spirits for me to research." The wind whips his bushy Aquarius hair, and he pushes it back from his eyes with one hand. "What about you?"

"I'm going to keep writing."

"You ought to. Let me know if I can help. Even if your article isn't selected, there are other opportunities for talented student writers. You have my e-mail address. Let's keep in touch."

I think he means it.

"I will," I say.

Jeremy meets me outside the dorm, and we get into Dirk's car. Soon, he will be gone, and I will drive back alone. These are our last moments together for I don't know how long, and I have no idea what to say. We pass wind-beaten Monterey cypress trees, their branches frozen like giant bonsai, and I remember 17-Mile Drive, that lone tree that derives its nourishment from the moisture of the rocks.

"What are you thinking?" His voice is rough.

"About your father's song." Sean Baylor had known something about parting. I wondered if he had written it before or after he had decided to disappear.

"What about the song?"

"I guess I'm trying to figure out how to say goodbye."

"Me, too." He pulls off on Highway 68 toward Salinas. "The airport isn't far."

"Darn."

He reaches for my hand. "I know."

I wonder if, in his mind, he is already leaving me behind, imagining what life will be like with his father in Dublin. That's my emotional Pisces Moon, feeling sorry for myself. I mentally tell it to butt out. A tearful parting scene isn't going to endear me to him.

The airport is smaller than I expected. We park on the first level and go upstairs to the Golden Tee restaurant. He orders a burger and fries.

"For breakfast?" I ask.

"This isn't just any day. What about you?"

"Coffee and toast."

"That's not very much," he says.

"This isn't just any day."

He leans over, whispers in my ear. "Your shirt is wrong-side-out."

"Oh no." I'm horrified. I was so exhausted when I woke up this morning that I didn't even notice the now-blatant black seams.

"Don't worry about it." He slides next to me in the booth. "I love the way you look. Logan, I love you."

My cheeks burn. I squeeze his fingers and am filled with more joy than I've ever felt, and more misery.

"What are we going to do?" I whisper.

"Just care about each other. And believe we can make it work." He gives me what I'm sure he thinks is a cheerful smile. "What do those on the astro plane say about love?"

"So, you're into astrology now, are you?"

"Let's just say I'm open to anything."

"Okay then. What we have here are Earth . . ." I point at him. ". . . And Air." I point at myself. "And we are going to be fine."

"Is that what you read?"

"Kind of." I blink to keep the tears away. "Close enough."

"We will be." He puts his arm around me, and we kiss in the booth, in front of a restaurant full of people.

Breakfast is over too soon, and it is time for him to board. We walk outside and hold hands as long as we can.

"Stay here," he says, when it's time for him to go on and for me to go back. "Watch my plane until it's gone. I'll be looking down at you until you're only a speck."

"I will." I wrap my arms around his neck and lift my lips to his ear, which is now as cold as the wind. "I love you, too."

That's the truth. It should make up for the fact that I fibbed a little earlier; it wasn't I didn't remember. I could have recited, by heart, every word of our horoscopes for today. *Heartbreak will be followed by redemption and a reawakening of spirit.*

Maybe so. But right now, I'm also thinking about what Mercedes said. *"Sometimes trying is good enough."* And I'm thinking about that Lone Cypress that digs in and survives.

"Wait for me then," he says.

"I will, I promise."

One more kiss. Then he hurries to catch up with the other passengers, takes a final look back down at me, and steps inside the plane. I stare at it and imagine him watching me from one of the tiny windows. I wave furiously to keep my mind from focusing on what is really happening.

The plane takes off, down the narrow runway, then up, up, growing smaller. It glints in the light, only a silver streak. I shade my eyes, blinded by the sun, but I can't turn away now. I keep watching and blinking until it disappears into the sky.

On the way home, I know what I must do next. The decision is simply made without any of my characteristic mulling. Still wearing the wrong-side-out shirt, I drive to the newspaper office.

The front security guard is still reading her magazine. "Sign in over there," she says.

I think about what Rik McNeil said in that fiery Aries way of his. *"Perhaps we're selected for a reason."*

Nobody is around this early. I walk to the place where the elevator used to be and press my cheek against the cold wall.

"It's okay, Richard," I say, although I might as well be speaking to Jeremy. "It is okay to leave. You're free." Tears fill my eyes.

The wall turns warm for a moment. I hear something that sounds like a sigh. Perhaps it is my imagination, perhaps not. It doesn't matter. In my mind, the wall disappears. The red enamel elevator doors part. Richard steps out in his uniform, smiles at me, nods and then walks smartly down the hall toward the back guard station. I follow him and watch the door swing open. A cold breeze cuts through me.

An old guy watching several surveillance cameras gets up

and closes the door. "Damn wind," he says. Then noticing me, he stops. "You need some help, Miss?" he asks. "Need to find someone?"

"I found what I needed," I say. "I'm leaving now."

As I begin to retrace my steps, the guard in front doesn't bother looking up. And that's okay as well.

I'm ready to go back now.

WHAT'S YOUR SUN SIGN?

JUST AS THE MOON ILLUMINATES THE DARKNESS OF THE SKY, THE MOON IN YOUR CHART SHEDS LIGHT ON YOUR DEEPEST PERSONAL NEEDS THAT MAY BE INVISIBLE EVEN TO YOU. WHILE THE SUN IS MASCULINE, THE MOON IS FEMININE. SHE RULES YOUR INTUITION AND EMOTIONS. THINK OF YOUR MOON AS BLENDING OR MODIFYING YOUR SUN SIGN'S POSITIVE OR NEGATIVE CHARACTERISTICS.

—Fearless Astrology

Aries: **March 21–22 to April 19–20**

Loves activity, Hates commitment, Can be unpredictable,
Daring, Impulsive, Temperamental

Taurus: **April 20–21 to May 20–21**

Loves stability, Hates being hurried,
Can be sweet-tempered, Shy, Willful, Inflexible

Gemini: **May 21–22 to June 21–22**

Loves information, Hates sitting still,
Can be persuasive, Flirty, Superficial, Frivolous

Cancer: **June 22–23 to July 22–23**

Loves nurturing, Hates change,
Can be sensitive, Caring, Moody, Whiny

Leo: **July 23–24 to Aug 23–24**
Loves attention, Hates being dominated,
Can be playful, Lively, Arrogant, Flamboyant

Virgo: **Aug 23–24 to Sept 23–24**
Loves routine, Hates lack of order,
Can be organized, Persistent, Critical, Complaining

Libra: **Sept 23–24 to Oct 23–24**

Loves social interaction, Hates being alone,
Can be diplomatic, Harmonious, Jealous, Manipulative

Scorpio: **Oct 24–25 to Nov 21–22**

Loves passion, Hates disloyalty,
Can be loyal, Protective, Suspicious, Obsessive

Sagittarius: **Nov 22–23 to Dec 21–22**

Loves freedom, Hates routine, Can be spontaneous,
Cheerful, fickle, unpredictable

Capricorn: **Dec 22–23 to Jan 19–20**

Loves being needed, Hates not having a plan, Can be witty,
hilarious, power-hungry, emotionally cold

Aquarius: **Jan 20–21 to Feb 18–19**

Loves analyzing everything, Hates getting emotional,
Can be independent, Curious, Detached, Eccentric

Pisces: **Feb 19–20 to March 20–21**

Loves daydreaming, Hates dealing with reality,
Can be intuitive, Empathetic, Reclusive, Spacey

HERE'S A SNEAK PEEK
AT THE NEXT BOOK IN THE
STAR CROSSED SERIES

GEMINI NIGHT

1

THE TAURUS-AQUARIUS RELATIONSHIP IS FULL OF BUMPS AND BRUISES. NOT THAT EITHER OF YOU MOVES ALL THAT FAST. TAURUS IS EARTH, AND AQUARIUS IS AIR. BECAUSE YOU ARE BOTH FIXED SIGNS, YOU ARE EACH CONVINCED YOU ARE RIGHT, WITH A CAPITAL R. WHEN TAURUS PUSHES, AQUARIUS STEPS BACK. IF YOU WANT THIS RELATIONSHIP TO WORK, THE BULL MUST STEP SOFTLY, AND THE WATER BEARER MUST REACH OUT.

—Fearless Astrology

erra Bella Beach had never seemed so lonely.

If I, Logan McRae, had paid more attention to Fearless Astrology, maybe I wouldn't be so miserable right now. Maybe I wouldn't have fallen for a Taurus. Jeremy had pushed. I had stepped back. And then I had stepped forward in a big way, a way that would and did change his life. Even though I was back home, and he was in Ireland, in my mind, I could still see the plane that carried him disappearing like a silver streak into the sky.

That had been almost three months ago. In spite of his e-mails from Ireland, I wasn't sure when or if this boy I couldn't stop thinking about would return. "I still love you," he told me each time we spoke. "Everything is the same." Only nothing was.

To make my life even more unsettled, my mother had arrived home from her golf tour the day I returned from my summer workshop. Then she and Dad had sat me down at the kitchen counter, no less, for the we-love-you-very-much talk. Translation: divorce.

Mom had assured me that she'd do her best to spend time at home when her schedule permitted. Dad had said that Gram Janie would move in after Christmas. Everything would be the same, they told me. Except nothing would be.

I had been sitting there, on a stool at the kitchen counter, staring at them and trying not to cry, when the phone rang.

"Logan? Hello. It's Henry Jaffa."

As if I hadn't recognized the voice.

"Hi," I squawked.

"Logan," he said. "I have what could be an amazing opportunity for you."

⁓⁓⁓

Monday morning in Terra Bella Beach. I had put on my black T-shirt with Writers Camp stenciled across it in purple. It would be nice to have a chest to go with it. Then I pulled on my yellow hoodie from the summer, remembering how I'd felt when Jeremy had held me.

I rode to school with my two best friends in Chili's Spyder. She and I sat in front. Paige leaned over from the backseat to catch our conversation above the music.

When I told them about the phone call from Jaffa and the possibility of working as an intern for CRUSH magazine, they both screamed.

"I knew it," Paige said.

Chili gave me a one-armed hug. "Oh Logan. You may have lost Jeremy, but you have a famous writer as a mentor."

"Thanks." My eyes stung.

"She hasn't lost Jeremy," Paige said in a soft Pisces voice. "Not necessarily."

"Right." Chili, like many born in her Gemini Sun sign, lied about as well as a five-year-old. "I just meant that having a famous author for a mentor is the best."

The music on the radio drilled into my head.

"Can we ditch Arianna Woods?" I asked.

"This song's better than her last." Chili pulled into the

Terra High parking lot and shut off the music. Then she drew back, and the look of concern on her face reminded me of Stella, her very hands-on Armenian mom.

"You're not moving to New York or anything, are you?"

"The magazine is published in San Francisco," I said. "I can commute."

They screamed again. Then, we got out of the car. For a moment, we just looked at each other. Chili in her cropped white sweater over a black tank and jeans, the sunlight glinting off her streaked hair. Paige in a shirt she'd designed herself, pale blue, to match her eyes, but something was different. Makeup. Was Paige really wearing makeup?

As we walked to class, Chili asked, "If CRUSH is in San Francisco, how will you be able to intern there? That's ninety minutes each way."

"I'm hoping the school, namely Ms. Snider, will go along with the plan. It's only one day a week."

Our hardworking Capricorn journalism teacher had cut me some slack last year when I was a sophomore, and I needed her support again.

We walked out of the parking lot, and as Chili and Paige headed for their first period classes, I started toward the journalism room.

Just then I noticed crazy Kat, the Aries cheerleader as she came around a corner. Her short, black hair was pushed back behind her ears. When she noticed me, she grinned.

"Hey, Logan. Did you hear about Nathan and Geneva?"

"No." I kept walking.

She ran up along side me. "They're going to Maui in

November."

"Good for them." I didn't turn to look at her, just kept on heading toward the journalism class.

"They'll be traveling with Nathan's family. His parents love Geneva."

Finally, I met her eyes. "And you're telling me this, because?"

She gave me a superior smirk. "Because I thought you'd want to know."

"What they do doesn't concern me, Kat," I said. "They're in college. I'm here. Besides, I have a new boyfriend."

"Oh, really? Who?"

"His name is Jeremy." Best not to mention that he was in Ireland, and that I had no idea when I would see him again.

"Oh." I could tell that I'd taken her by surprise and that she was trying to come up with a fiery Aries insult. "How'd you manage that? Did you use astrology on him?"

As if it were a magic trick that would snag me any guy I wanted.

"In a way." That should give her something to gossip about. I didn't care.

Ms. Snider stepped out of the classroom. Ever the perfect Capricorn in her crisp little brown tunic and cream-colored turtleneck, she looked hot. The rumor was that she was dating my English teacher, Mr. Franklin, but they hadn't gone public with it.

"Good morning," she said.

"Hi, Ms. Snider. Um, could I talk to you for a minute?"

"About Henry Jaffa?" Her expression got a little less

friendly. "You know I'm proud of you, Logan, but you should-n't have asked Jaffa to pressure me."

"What are you talking about? I didn't ask him to do any-thing."

"Really? Then why did he contact me last night?"

"I swear I don't know."

"Well, he called the superintendent." Color rose along her cheeks. "As you can imagine, I don't appreciate such manip-ulation from anyone, not even a well-known writer."

"Henry Jaffa is not a manipulator," I said before I remem-bered that I was talking back to a teacher. "He's very straightforward, and he's not the type to pull strings."

"Well, he's certainly pulling them, or trying to."

Kat stared openly, no doubt taking mental notes for Geneva.

"Could we go inside?" I asked Snider. "I'd like to talk to you without an audience."

"Don't flatter yourself." Kat said under her breath, but she didn't move.

Snider seemed to take it in. "All right. Shall we walk down the hall?"

Good idea. Students would be filling the journalism room any minute.

"I didn't know that Mr. Jaffa contacted you," I told her. "All I said to him is that I would need the approval of the school. Maybe that's why he phoned the superintendent, and since you're my journalism teacher . . ."

"Whatever the reason, I got called, at home, on a Sunday and hit with considerable pressure from a famous writer."

"I am sorry if I caused any of that," I said. "I was just so excited about the internship. If you can help me get it, I'll make up the time."

"Are you still involved with that astrology stuff?"

Yes, Capricorn, and don't be so true-to-your-sign frosty about it. "I am," I said. "It's what I used last spring when everything here was in such an uproar." Not to mention your reputation. I didn't say it, but I could tell by her expression that she understood.

"What happened last spring was all about your courage and your intelligence," she said. "And, yes, I know how much you want to believe otherwise."

"But what does that have to do with my internship?" I asked.

"Only this." She lowered her voice. "Henry Jaffa."

"What about him?"

"His beliefs, the subjects he writes about. All of that paranormal stuff." She paused in the hall. "You're a good kid, Logan. I want you to learn to rely on yourself and not on magic."

"Astrology isn't magic," I said. "And CRUSH is a teen magazine. I know the superintendent will go along with the internship if you approve."

"Okay," she said. "I will do that on two conditions."

"Anything," I managed to say.

"First, you can go to the magazine only one day a week."

"No problem. That's the way the internship is set up."

"Second, you have to promise me that you'll stay away from astrology."

"Totally away?"

"Away," she said. "Promise me that you will not use it to run your life."

That was easy. Astrology didn't run my life. It enhanced and expanded my life.

"It's a deal," I told her.

NOTES TO SELF

It's happened. It's going to take a lot of extra work, and I'll have a lot of make-up assignments, but I now have approval to intern at the magazine every Friday, starting four days from tonight. The moon will be in Gemini, meaning that my Air sign communication skills should be at their best. So, yes, I am thinking about astrology again right now, but not in a magical way. In a hopeful way.

Bonnie Hearn Hill is a Gemini, a full-time writer, and a former editor for a daily newspaper. She is the author of INTERN and five other adult thriller novels. She teaches writing in her hometown of Fresno, California and on Writer's Digest Online. She also mentors writers and speaks at numerous writing conferences. Read more about Bonnie and your astrological sign at: www.bonniehearnhill.com